DI

VINCENT & EVE
BOOK ONE

RISING

JESSICA RUBEN

JessicaRubenBooks, LLC
229 E. 85th street
P.O. box 1596
New York New York 10028

Copyright © 2018 Jessica Ruben
Paperback ISBN: 978-1-7321178-1-5
E-Book ISBN: 978-1-7321178-0-8
Printed in the United States of America

Visit my website at www.jessicarubenauthor.com

Cover art design by Okay Creations
Formatting by A Books Mind
Editing by Billi Joy Carson at Editing Addict
Editing by Ellie at LoveNBooks
Beta Editing by Hot Tree Editing
Publicity from Autumn at Wordsmith Publicity

CONTENTS

CHAPTER 1

Oak desks, scuffed from years of abuse and handy knife work, stand single file in the back of the dingy public library. Curled up in a dark wooden chair, with elbows resting on the etched wood, I read the newest novel recommended by my teacher, Ms. Levine. I lift my head for a moment when my gaze lands on the nearly opaque second-story window, grimy from New York City pollution.

My eyes widen. "Oh shit," I say out loud, my voice ringing through the empty room. Eyes registering the darkness outside, my stomach liquefies with dread. I check my cell to confirm the time—it's ten fifteen.

Grabbing my ratty backpack off the floor, I slide the book inside and zip it closed as quickly as my shaking hands allow. Throwing it over my shoulder, I rush out the front door and make it to the dimly lit bus stop, just as the M-6 pulls in. I walk up the steps and swipe my metro card at the kiosk by the driver.

Noticing an empty seat by the window in the second row, I walk over, squeezing my small five-foot-one frame past the woman sitting in the aisle seat. She sighs as if annoyed, leaning back in an attempt to maintain distance.

Wearing green scrubs, she has exhaustion written all over her drawn face. I take my seat and lick my dry lips, turning my gaze to the window.

As the bus approaches my stop on the Lower East Side, I raise the hood of my black sweatshirt. Anonymity is key in my neighborhood—particularly as a lone female walking at night. I live in the Blue Houses, a New York City housing project recently dubbed by the *Post* as "the hellhole houses." The nickname came as no surprise, as the complex is dilapidated and crime-ridden. It's common knowledge that cops always enter the building with their guns drawn, assuming that all tenants are packing weapons. To make matters worse, two gangs, the Snakes and the Cartel, are in a turf war for rights to push crack, the preferred pastime for many Blue House residents. The gutters run blood daily. Although I'm born and raised here, my time spent with my head inside the books has left me with street smarts that are at best decent, and at worst delinquent. My older sister Janelle reminds me of this constantly, and in this moment, I'm proving her right.

I'm so close to the building now, only about nine hundred feet away from the front yard. My eyes scan the eerily empty streets that, during daylight hours, are full of commotion. I force myself to stay calm by focusing on this morning when my sister's friends chatted about who's banging who, while old-school Tupac blasted on someone's iPhone speakers. I pull the hoodie closer to my head as my mind revists to the scene.

***

"Jem got pregnant—"

"Ohhhhh shit! No way! No fuckin' way! That poor mama of hers—"

"—I heard that Mark is gonna kick Sean's ass. He owes him money, but who's gonna pay that debt? Everyone knows he spends all his money on his—"

I shift my focus from the gossip mill to the girls jumping rope in front of me, crisscrossing and jumping with ease.

"Yo Eve, you listenin'?" I turn my head to Vania, one perfectly plucked eyebrow raised in frustration.

I plaster a smile on my face. "Sorry, what?"

She rolls her dark brown eyes. "Girl, you've got to get your head outta la-la land!" I flush with embarrassment; this isn't the first time I've been accused of spacing out. "I asked you if you saw Jason. He told Jennifer that he thinks you're: Hot. As. Fuck."

I shrug my shoulders. "Nah. I'm not really interested." She looks at me like I've got a screw loose in my head, and I immediately wish I said something other than the truth. Jason is tall with jet-black hair, blue eyes, and totally tatted from his head to his ankles. Most girls would give almost anything to be with a man like that. And while my eyes recognize his relative attractiveness, he doesn't affect me the way he does everyone else.

"I love your shade of lipstick!" My voice is full of forced enthusiasm, but I'm hoping to divert the conversation.

"It's called Honey Love. It's MAC." She purses her lips together, showing off the creamy nude shade.

I nod my head, relieved that the conversation of Jason is now behind us. "That's cool. I gotta tell Janelle to try it on me sometime."

Warmth fills her face. "Yeah, baby girl. And with your tan skin, pouty lips, and huge brown eyes…shiiiit. You'll have guys lining up." I blush, uncomfortable with the praise.

I turn to my sister, who is all long blond hair and legs for miles. While I share her small nose and bow-shaped lips, our physical similarities are minimal. Janelle is five-foot-seven and statuesque, whereas I'm short and curvy.

Vania clears her throat, rummaging through her purse. "Here. Let me put some on you." She takes out a lipstick and lipliner from her huge black tote bag that looks more like a suitcase than a purse, and gets to work on my lips. When she's finished, she leans back, seemingly pleased.

"Yo, Janelle. Take a look at baby sister over here." Janelle turns her head, smiling as she takes me in.

"You're smokin'. Je-sus!" She winks at me before turning back to Vania. "What color is that? Honey Love?"

"Of course, you know, you bitch!" They laugh together, Vania turning her attention back to Janelle. "I read that Mario uses this new color mix on Kim Kardashian—"

I slide up closer to them, trying to listen to their conversation, but everything they say goes in one ear and out the other. I'm the listener. The dreamer. The girl with her head in a book at all times. But even I know that in order to survive here, I've got to belong. Loners get picked on and picked off. But Janelle? She's the social butterfly. The girl everyone loves. And if not for her, I'd probably be floating in the Hudson by now. I move my body closer to the group, doing my best to fit in.

***

I stumble on a hard piece of trash on the sidewalk, bringing my focus back to the present. The unnaturally silent air has alarm bells ringing in my head. I wonder if the gangs are roaming hard tonight. I look to the park adjacent to the Blue Houses, trying to find the regular late-night junkies. It's the most secure place for people to do drugs, as the cops never make regular patrols; apparently, they're too busy answering 911 calls. I take a sharp breath; the entire park is seemingly abandoned.

I tighten my hold on the straps of my backpack and quicken my pace, focusing on making it to the front door of my building. My heart rate increases as my imagination spirals. Maybe someone was shot earlier, and now everyone is home scared? Did someone die? Someone must have died. Is there blood on the sidewalk? There's blood. I know it. Fear takes hold, choking me. For all the laughter and friendly neighborhood vibes during the day, the reality is the Blue Houses are a deadly place to live.

When I hear the telltale *hiss* of the Snakes, the blood in my veins turns cold. I run as fast as I can, but the *hissing* only increases in volume. Risking a glance over my shoulder, I see a group close behind me. Janelle's voice enters my mind, *"If you run, you'll look scared. And looking scared makes you more vulnerable."* Even though my heart is pounding like a steel drum into my rib cage, I force myself to slow down. My legs beg to sprint forward, but showing fear isn't an option.

I make it a few more feet when they circle me, blocking any path of escape. My mouth opens, poised to scream, but my throat locks shut. It's so dark, but the shadows of the streetlamps bring their red and black colors into focus. My body quakes from my fingertips down into my toes. Dropping my head, I stare at the ground as the lieutenant of the Snakes moves in front of me. Focusing on his black steel-toe boots, a cold sweat breaks out on my forehead.

It's Carlos. As a kid, he used to torture and kill mice in the stairwell and leave them as threats for people by their front doors. He's been in and out of prison more times than I can count. In my mind's eye, I can see the blue teardrops tatted under his left eye down to the corner of his thin lips, each oval bead signifying a kill.

"Take that hood off. I wanna get a good look at you." His voice is low and menacing. I move to lift my head, pausing at his muscular bare chest. I

5

shudder, making eye contact with his black-and-red snake tattoo. It peeks over his right shoulder, tongue hissing between two pointy white fangs like a beast from hell.

When Carlos sees I'm not doing as he demanded, he throws off my hood, roughly grabbing my chin and forcing my head straight. I can smell his rancid breath as he fists my hair in his hand. Staring at my face, he nods with what looks like appreciation.

"We found something good tonight, boys," he chuckles as if he's found a new toy he can't wait to play with. Bile rises up my throat as his smile widens.

My eyes dart from side to side as my breathing turns erratic. I'm fresh meat, and these animals are in it for the kill. Screaming won't make a difference. How many times have I heard yelling outside my bedroom window, but never thought to help the victim? Countless. Maybe it's karma. Maybe I deserve this for all the times I dropped my head and tried not to get involved. If I only listened to Janelle and made sure not to be alone on the streets at night—

Carlos steps back, pulling a cigarette from behind his ear and placing it between his lips. Taking a black lighter from his front pocket, he flicks it on and off, letting the fire burn at his will. Bringing the flame to the end of his cigarette, he takes a hard pull, turning the tip into a shining ember. With an exhale, smoke wafts around his face and blends into the night. He stands silently, assessing every detail of my trembling body.

"Looks like we're gonna have some fun," he laughs as his boys cackle in delight. My jaw slackens as my mind searches for an escape. If I can't physically get out of this, maybe I can force my mind to move elsewhere.

He grabs my upper arm. I can feel the bruising take shape as he turns me around forcefully, dragging me like a rag doll toward the Blue Houses. The others trail behind us, reminding me with every step that I have nowhere to go. Nowhere to hide. Nowhere to run.

Pushing through the front door of the building, we stop in front of what I always thought was a storage room. Carlos stuffs his hand in his pocket, removing a key. Shoving it inside the keyhole, he throws the door open, using his free hand to push me into the room. I trip over my own feet, the cement greeting me as I fall to my hands and knees. He flips a switch and the light casts a shadow below me. I lift my head and see a tiny barred window above a small bed. I look to my right, only to see a kitchenette with a round table surrounded by plastic chairs. Carlos bends down, grabbing me by the neck and pulling me up to face him. I want to scream, but my throat is closed. I see the exhilaration in his eyes and briefly wonder if death isn't the better option.

He loosens his hold on my neck, and I take deep, but shaky, inhales. The moment I catch my breath, he slaps me hard across the face. My body gets the message—he's the one in control. I open and close my mouth, shutting my eyes and willing my brain to tune out and turn off.

He grabs my chin. "I've been seeing you around. And get this? You're just the one we need for tonight. You see, we've got lots of energy we need to burn off after where we've been." He licks his lips and I can see the dull yellow of his teeth. "I know you like to hide in those baggy clothes with those books in your hands, but I think it's about time you show us what you've got goin' on underneath all that shit." He laughs, pulling out a fresh cigarette and lighting it up. "Take your clothes off for us, and do it niiiice and slow. I think we're all in the mood for a little live show tonight."

A chair is pulled out and I lift my head to the sound. I make eye contact with one of the guys and his head snaps back in recognition. "Oh shit, Carlos, that's Janelle's little sister." It's Jason. His hair is styled in an undercut, buzzed on the sides and long on top. I'm shaking so badly it takes me a second to realize he's staring right at me, waiting for a reply.

"Y-Yeah," I stammer. "I'm J-J-Janelle's sister."

He shrugs casually at the guys. "Let's get rid of her. She's harmless. You know Janelle; she's the one who does all the old ladies' hair for free, and—"

Carlos throws a hand up in the air, silencing him. "Rid of her? Like, shoot her in the head?" He cocks his head to the side in question and the blood drains from my face. "Nah. I don't think I want to kill her just yet. Fuck her virgin brains out, yeah. Let all you guys take a turn when I'm done, hell yeah. Afterwards, you can kill her if you still want." He smiles and grabs my hand, lifting it above my head. I shut my eyes as he twirls me in a slow circle, showing me off to his crew. I hear wolf whistles and try to turn my thoughts into white noise.

A scratchy voice from the side of the room starts up. "Don't rough her up too much at first. I want her to have some fight left when I get my turn."

Tears drip from my eyes, burning as they fall down the sides of my face. "I'll d-d-do anything. Just let me go. Please…" I beg, dropping down to my knees and lifting my hands in prayer. "I'll do anything you want, but I don't want to die."

"Anything, huh? Get up," he commands. I stand on wobbly feet as Carlos grins maliciously. "Ah, you take directions. That's good. Very good." He lifts his steel toe boot, kicking me in the stomach. I double over.

Carlos bends low, grabbing my hair to lift my head and bringing his lips to my ear, his voice a dark growl. "Let me give you a piece of advice. Shut the FUCK up and take what we're all about to give you. You may even enjoy it after the first few times." He puts his nose to my neck, smelling me deeply as he presses a sharp object against my side. My eyes widen; I feel the cold sharp edge of a blade drifting from my ribs up to my chest.

"Listen to what I tell you. Don't want to mess up that gorgeous face. But…" My breathing stops. "I will, IF you don't do as I say. You want to live? Shut up and take it." He moves his knife back to his pocket. "Strip."

He chuckles.

I oblige.

I remove every layer of clothing and stand crumpled. My shoulders are curled down and my arms cover my bare breasts. He thrusts my arms away.

His dirty fingertips grope my intimate parts as if he owns them. The body I thought belonged to me is now on loan. Finally, my mind separates from my body and floats away. But Carlos, unwilling to let me go in body or mind, pulls the cigarette out of his mouth and presses it against my shoulder.

I let out a scream from the burn.

He laughs.

Carlos turns to his boys, rubbing his hands together in eagerness. "I'm gonna make sure she's good enough for you all, first." They all chuckle at the joke, while one of them stares at me with rapt attention and a look of utter excitement.

"Poker—"

A cabinet opens and shuts.

The smell of old and wet laundry.

I close my eyes.

"Open your eyes and look at me!" Yelling, he grabs my neck to face him, forcing me to watch his ministrations.

My eyes connect with his, nothing but evil lurks in his depths.

I'm thrust forward, face down on the bed. I hear pants unzipping and falling to the floor. I hold my breath. If I hold it long enough, will I die?

"Yo, snake charmers! Cartel is In. The. Houssssse!" Voices and laughter radiate straight through the barred window and into the room. Carlos pauses, turning toward the glass and screaming, "We're coming MOTHERFUCK-ERS!"

My body shakes uncontrollably. I can hear him pull his pants back up, heaving. "The FUCK? If the Cartel is looking for a fight tonight, we'll give em' one!"

I dare to crack my eyes open, watching as they nod to each other. The rivalry between the Snakes and the Cartel is vicious. While the Cartel has fewer members, they make up for less manpower with intense and frequent bloodshed.

I'm in a state of shock, watching them pull weapons from their pants. Am I going to die? I shut my eyes again, moaning.

"Yo!" Carlos slaps my ass so hard I bite my lip, tasting copper. "Don't think you're off the hook, bitch. I got a glimpse, and now I want in. I'm coming back for you." He raises his gun and thrusts it into my mouth. I choke as he pushes it deeper down. Tearing it out, he nods—his version of a guarantee.

Seconds later, I feel warm hands on my naked back. "Open your eyes and get up." The voice is soft but urgent. Jason is on his knees by the bed, my clothes in his hands. "Put your clothes on, and get out of here!" he whispers loudly.

Somehow, I stand. I'm a machine, clothing myself like I've done millions of times before. He has the decency to turn his head as I put one foot and then the other into my underwear. As I slide my T-shirt and sweatshirt over my head, I realize I am no longer the priority to these criminals. If there is a time to run, it's now.

I take my bag and run out of the room with a speed I didn't know I was capable of. Opening the heavy stairwell door and running up the steps, I take two at a time as sweat pours down my temples. Are they after me? Are they coming? I want to turn my head back to see if they're behind me, but my fear won't let me turn around.

I hear cursing and some screams, but all the sounds are muffled by the whooshing sound in my ears. The stairs seem to vibrate with the sound of gunshots. Have I been shot? Adrenalin mixed with confusion pumps through my veins as I jet up the darkened stairwell; the lights are all out on the third floor, and it feels like I'm running through a black hole. My heart pounds into my throat.

In a blink, I'm back inside my empty apartment, staring in a trance at my gray threadbare living-room couch. I look at my feet and realize I'm barefoot. Oh shit, I'm going to need to buy a new pair of sneakers. I wonder if there's any in my size at the thrift store.

Turning toward my bedroom door, my mind registers the crack down the center. I briefly remember one of my mom's old boyfriends throwing a vase against it, splitting the wood. I walk into my room like a zombie and complete my nightly routine of brushing my teeth, washing my face with soap and scalding hot water, and changing into a clean pair of pajamas. In the recesses of my mind, I know what just happened to me is horrifying, but I keep telling myself if I just act normal, maybe it'll all just go away.

Before getting into my bed, I kneel on the floor, fisting my worn-out navy comforter in my hands. Prayers tumble out of my mouth to God, begging him to get me out of here before Carlos finds me. All at once, I feel punched in the gut. I run to the toilet, dropping my head into the bowl and emptying all the contents of my stomach.

Are they going to come for me tonight? Should I hide? I shut the bathroom door and curl up in the fetal position by the toilet, too afraid to go back into my bedroom where there's a window.

What feels like seconds later, I hear the front door open and close. As footfalls get closer to the bathroom door, my chest constricts, my mouth gaping open and poised to scream.

"Eve, are you in the bathroom? Get out, I need to wash up!" Janelle throws the door open and looks down at me on the floor, momentarily confused.

She gives me a once over. "You look like shit, girl." Her voice is quiet and laced with concern. "What are you doing in the bathroom? Are you sick?" I hear her, but can't manage a reply. She squats down, placing the back of her hand on my forehead.

"Holy shit, Eve, you're burning up! And your face is pale as hell. You think it's food poisoning or something? Let me get you some meds." She helps me up off the floor and walks me to my bed, letting me lean on her as we walk. A few minutes later, she drops two pills into my hand. I put them on my tongue when she hands me a glass of water. I swallow the medicine and a few minutes later, I'm plunged into sleep.

CHAPTER 2

I wake up to the sound of the shower running and pipes groaning. I shut my eyes again, savoring the few minutes of relative quiet before Janelle comes back into our room. When I hear the water turn off, dread pools in my stomach. I can barely get enough air into my lungs to complete a solid breath. Every part of me wants to pretend like last night didn't happen, but I need to tell her if I want to stay alive. Oblivious to my anxiety levels, she shuffles into the room and hops into my small single bed, a fluffy pink towel draped around her tall and thin frame. She presses a hand against my head, checking my temperature.

"You're getting me soaked," I complain, my voice a morning rasp.

"I'm glad you're up! And I guess your fever is gone. It must have been food poisoning, right?" She hops off the bed and opens our shared closet, pulling out a white tank top and skinny jeans, getting ready for work. She's a hair stylist at the salon at Bergdorf Goodman. It's a job any girl in her industry would kill for. Most of the salon's clients are celebrities or rich uptown girls with trust funds; they book months in advance for a cut or highlights, ranging upwards of three-hundred dollars. After sliding on her jeans and a lacy white bra, she looks down at her phone, smiling at whatever she's seeing. Her face lights up.

"Oh my God, Eve." She turns to me with a smile and then brings her gaze back to the phone. "Guess who's coming into the salon today? Gwyneth!" She jumps up and down. "Louis just texted me." She looks down at herself, eyebrows low. "Shit! I need to change into something better than this." Re-opening our closet, she rummages through clothes.

"Janelle..." I start. She swivels her head, turning to me.

"What is it?" she asks nonchalantly, pressing a navy blouse against her chest and staring at herself in our long mirror.

"Something really bad happened. We need to talk." I drop my head nervously. When I look back up, I see anxiety clear in her eyes.

Placing her phone beside her, she sits next to me. "What's going on?"

I have to swallow a few times, but eventually, find the strength to tell her about the Snakes. She sits in silence until I'm completely done with every horrifying detail. It's agony to recount the story, but I need to tell her the truth. I need her help.

"Oh, Eve." Her face crumbles and tears well in her eyes. She draws me into her chest as we both start to cry.

"The Snakes." She sobs. "Those guys are psychotic!"

"I know I messed up big time, Janelle." Embarrassment mixed with agony blazes through me. I'm old enough to know better. I was literally saved by a stroke of luck. I could have been raped and beaten. Left for dead.

"Janelle," I sob. "It's all my fault. If I had just listened to you and didn't lose track of time, none of this would have happened." I curl into her side, bawling uncontrollably.

She pulls back, staring at me hard. "Eve, stop this. This is not your fault. Do you hear me? It's NOT your fault. Walking home late at night does not mean that anyone has the right to take you or to touch you against your will." Her words echo in my head. "I never want to hear you talk like this. We live in a dangerous place and God knows you do everything you can to stay under the radar. But you have to live, right?" She pulls me closer to her body, holding me together when it feels as though I'm being torn apart. "I'll figure out how to get you out of this. He won't come back for you, all right? We'll figure it out together."

A memory rushes to the forefront of my head. "I forgot to tell you, but Jason was there." I stare off into space, remembering how he thrust my clothes at me and practically begged me to run.

"Jason Mendes?" A half smile forms on her lips and my face immediately falls.

"Don't even think about it, Janelle!" I hiccup, knowing what she's insinuating.

She has the decency to drop her head for a moment. "Come on, Eve. Chill out. He isn't one of them, just a hang-around. His mom is on the sixth floor and sick with cancer. I do her hair sometimes and met him when I was over there. He deals some drugs for the Snakes on occasion, but nothing really too serious. I think he's a mechanic or something, actually. Anyway, maybe if you were closer to him," she says, raising her eyebrows at the word *closer*. "They'd leave you alone. Wasn't Vania saying the other day that he's into you?"

"No," I tell her, my voice shaking. "Why don't you go out with him? If he was with you, he'd probably protect me too, right?"

"Everyone knows I'm with Leo these days. Otherwise, I'd hit him up in a heartbeat." She winks at me in an attempt to lighten the mood.

She and Leo have a crazy relationship. One minute he's the best guy ever, the next she'd be screaming at the top of her lungs and cursing the day he was born. I haven't met him yet, but I'm not too eager considering all the drama he causes. Just the thought of him has me rolling my eyes.

She looks at me and huffs. "Stop being so judgmental, Eve. I see the look on your face and it isn't pretty."

"It's not unwarranted judgment. The guy takes you on an emotional roller coaster on a weekly basis! You deserve better than him." I get out of bed, agitated and feeling weirdly hollow.

"Unwarranted judgment?" she repeats, standing up tall. "Okay, Miss Big-Shot attorney." Her condescending voice is like a kick to the chest. "Anyway, he cares about me." She lifts her head up.

"A man who cares about you won't put you through that," I sass, surprised at my tone.

She places a hand on her hip and shifts her weight to one leg. "Did your books teach you that? Because one stupid make-out session with Juan doesn't qualify you as a relationship guru. And clearly, you don't exactly have the best intuition, huh?"

My heart sinks.

"I—" My face crumbles and her face falls in regret as she steps forward, throwing her arms around me. I lean into her, my tears running like a faucet.

She sighs, holding me by the shoulders. "Look. I'm sorry, okay? I shouldn't have said that. Especially after what you've just been through. I know jumping into a man's bed for protection is the last thing you'd ever do. But girl, we've got to figure something out!" Her voice is desperate as she pulls me back into her chest, rubbing my back. I keep crying, and she continues to shush me gently.

When I finally catch my breath, she sits us both down at the table. "I don't want you worrying about Carlos. I have so much goodwill in this building, did you forget? I'll cash in a favor. Someone will talk to him and tell him you're completely off limits, okay?" I manage to nod my head. "You know these morons have short attention spans. One second, it's all about you and the next, they're on to someone or something else." I look up at her and see hope shining through her glassy eyes.

As a favor to some of the older ladies in the building, Janelle sometimes spends her time cutting and coloring their hair for free. Especially when the elevator is dead, it becomes too hard for older people to take the steps and leave the building. Even if they are strong enough to walk all the way downstairs, most of them are afraid of taking the stairwell all alone, and rightly so. With the lights always going out, bad shit will often go down in there.

People are always looking to repay Janelle for her kindness. Usually, it's in the form of home cooking. But maybe Janelle is right. Maybe she really can have someone talk to Carlos, and he'll leave me alone.

"Now go take a shower," she instructs. "You have work at Angelo's today, right? It's good for you to get out of here and clear your head. We'll take the subway uptown together and you'll call me before you come home so I can meet you."

"O-kay," I manage to stutter.

She bites her lip, and I can tell there is more she wants to say. "Don't get mad with what I'm about to tell you, because I know you won't like it." She lets out a loud exhale. "I think you need to consider talking to Angelo about what happened."

"No!" I reply vehemently. "I'm not talking about this with him. If he got the Borignone family involved, I'd be bringing a shit storm on myself." I angrily wipe the tears off my face with my fingers, feeling some scratches on my face. My stomach churns.

Janelle clears her throat, snapping me back into the moment. "Yeah, but what if my connections can't control Carlos? We've got to think of a backup plan."

"If I let the Borignones help me, I'll be indebted to them. I can't get involved. Once I start owing people, I may as well be dead. You know Antonio—no favor is free."

She sighs. "Okay. Let's see what I can do first." She hugs me again as I walk out of the room with my head down.

Entering the bathroom, I tell myself Janelle will be able to fix this for me. My tears are now laced with relief, because she's here and has my back. She'll talk to someone. She'll make sure the Snakes don't bother me again. I'm not alone in this. I take my clothes off carefully, making sure not to look at myself in the mirror. Just the thought of being naked sickens me. This body I've been given is up for grabs, belonging to anyone stronger than me who wants it. I turn on the water extra hot, practically scalding myself as I step under the spray. I want to clean Carlos' fingerprints from my body.

I know when Janelle mentioned the Borignone family, she did it because they are probably the only ones who could actually kill Carlos and get away with it. The Borignones are the most notorious crime family on the East Coast. They do everything from trafficking illegal drugs and guns to owning half of New York City real estate and small businesses—from cleaners and pawnshops to strip clubs and gas stations, all under their control. They even own Angelo's Pawn, the shop I work at. But turning to them to fix this for me has to be my last resort. Being in debt to the Borignones would be a nightmare. My mom has been under their thumb for years, and Janelle and I have sworn on our lives we'd never fall into their trap.

On the other hand, Angelo is an associate with the big boss's ear. There's no doubt if I told Angelo what happened, he'd arrange to have Carlos's neck snapped before I got my weekly paycheck.

My mom got me the job with Angelo two years ago. She's a stripper at a gentleman's club on the West Side—owned, of course, by none other than the big boss, Antonio Borignone. When I was looking for a weekend job, Antonio told my mom about an opening at Angelo's Pawn. I was scared as hell because saying *no* to Antonio was not an option. Working for Angelo was frightening at first, yet he turned out to be one of the best guys I've ever known. He lets me read and study when the shop is quiet, and in return, I write essays for his son Alex, who goes to some fancy prep school. I've read and written essays on some of the most amazing classic literature of all time. Last year, I asked Angelo if I could see my grades from the papers I write, and he now brings me the marked-up essays from Alex's professors. I've tried to learn from my errors to make my writing better, and according to his teacher's remarks, it looks like I'm truly growing as a writer.

After getting dressed, I walk into our tiny kitchenette where Janelle passes me a coffee with two packets of Splenda. "I'm gonna do my makeup, then we'll hit it. You okay?" I nod my head quietly and move to sit in the small folding chair at the kitchen table. Staring out the window with my coffee sitting in front of me, I think about my mother. I wonder how long it's been since I saw her last. A few weeks? A month, maybe? I look around the kitchenette, remembering the days when my mom would only be gone for a few days, but it felt like forever.

***

"Girls, let's go shopping!" my Mom squeals from the doorway, clapping her hands together. We turn our heads and smile in surprise; our mama is home!

She's been gone for three and a half days. Janelle and I jump off our chairs and run to the front door, greeting her with tight hugs around the waist.

"Mama, can we go to Toys'R'Us? There's this new scooter I wanna get!" Janelle lifts her hands in prayer, blinking her baby-blue eyes that people always gush over.

"Today we can do anything you girls want! My bank account is ready for action! I met this guy. His name is Antonio Borignone—and he's rich and gorgeous! He says he'll take the best care of me! And I just know he's telling the truth!" Her smile is huge and scary, bigger than usual. Janelle turns to me, happiness bursting out of her face, and I push the funny feeling I have in my belly away.

My mom starts talking so quickly, my head is spinning. "First, let's go to the toy store. Then, let's get McDonald's. Or, no, let's go to one of those fancy places in SoHo! We'll go get our hair and nails done! Janelle, you could use some blond in your hair like me. But not Eve, her hair is too dark." She turns to both of us, touching our faces. "God, my girls are so beautiful. Not as beautiful as me of course, but you can hope one day, maybe!"

I notice how fast her lashes are fluttering. I put my finger on my eye to feel my own lashes; do mine move like that too?

My gaze lands to a stack of books in the corner of the room, all of which I've read too many times. "Mama, can we also stop at the bookshop? There are so many books I want to buy!" I jump up and down a few times, unable to contain my excitement.

She swallows hard as her eyes darken, and I realize I just made a big mistake. She moves her long blond hair to one shoulder, pressing her lips together. "What does a six-year-old kid care about books, Eve? No books! Do you hear me? You can't be filling your head with that shit. Who taught you to fuckin' read, anyway?" She turns her body away from me, focusing on my sister. "Janelle, was it you?" I drop my head, fingering the holes in my leggings.

"No, Mama. She taught herself," Janelle replies in a quiet voice.

"Eve, what you trying to be, huh? I refuse to raise an uppity girl," she huffs. "You think you're better than everyone else around you? You think you deserve more? You'd leave this place behind without a second thought if you could, huh?" I stay quiet, not sure what I'm supposed to say. Wanting more, or better, than *this* isn't a good thing.

After a few moments of silence, I look up at Janelle, terrified I may have angered our mom badly enough to ruin our day. She gives me a tiny head nod and I finally bring my eyes back to my mother.

"Well. You got anything to say for yourself, Doctor Eve?" She laughs. I keep my mouth shut. Being a doctor isn't a good thing.

She steps up to me, putting her long, manicured fingers in my hair, pulling one spiral curl down and watching it bounce back into place. "Dark and curly, just like that asshole," she huffs.

She looks around the room, eyes moving from corner to corner. "Girls, are you turning this place into a pigsty?" Her voice is high-pitched and loud. "The place looks nasty. Eve, clean the kitchen." She watches as I open the closet door and pull out some cleaning supplies. The moment my hands touch the bleach, she lets out a sigh of relief.

She places a hand on her bony hip, facing me. "While me and Janelle wash up for our day, you take care of this." She gestures around the room with her hands. I look up at her again and nod my head. If I can just make her happy with the cleaning, maybe she'll love me more and stop leaving all the time.

"And IF you get it all done in time, then maybe…" her voice trails off and I inhale, hoping. "Then maybe," she repeats, "you'll come with us." I exhale.

My mom struts into her bedroom, slamming the door behind her. Janelle is still next to me, squeezing my hand three times. It's our secret signal for a promise. "I'll help you clean up. We'll all go out together."

"Okay, Janelle," I whisper, dropping my head.

"Don't be sad, baby girl. We're going to have the best day ever." I shrug, hoping things will look up.

She bends down low, placing her lips at my ear to tell me a secret. I stand on my tippy-toes, wanting to make sure I hear every word. Janelle's lips graze over my ear, her warm breath giving me the chills. "Don't tell Mom, but if you want, we can return some toys when she leaves and use the money for books."

"Really?" I throw my hands over my mouth, trying not to laugh too loudly. "You're right. This is going to be the best day ever!"

"Shh! Let's just get this cleaning done before she comes out." Janelle picks up the folding chair from the kitchen table and places it in front of the sink so I can climb up to reach the faucet.

We put the box of Cheerios in the cupboard and then scrub our breakfast bowls side by side. We had our cereal this morning with water, which I really don't like. We've been out of milk for weeks.

When we finish cleaning up, we walk together into our tiny bedroom. I love how we share. I don't like to be alone.

Janelle turns to me, her eyes full of promise. "One day, Eve, I'm gonna get a job and make sure we always have food on the table. And you're gonna be a doctor or a lawyer with that big brain of yours. Don't listen to Mama, okay? You keep on reading. We're gonna get out of this place." I quietly nod as she kisses me on the head and walks to the bathroom. I change into a pair of leggings without too many holes, hoping my mom won't be embarrassed by me.

After a day of nonstop shopping, we finally get back home with bags full of toys and our hair done up in curls and our nails shining with color. Janelle and I drop onto the couch, exhausted.

"Mama, can we watch a movie tonight?" Janelle asks. I smile wide, hoping my mom says *yes*. Because Janelle is thirteen, she always knows the best movies to watch.

My mom ignores the question and looks down, checking her phone and smiling. "Girls, Mama needs to go out for a little bit. Take good care of your toys!" And just like that, she's gone again.

***

As we got older, we learned that when Mom was happy, the supermarket needed to be our first stop. She'd walk with us up and down the aisles, laughing and playing supermarket sweep. We'd buy up every dry good we could fit into our cart. Fresh food wasn't smart since it ultimately went bad, but we'd take lots of canned fruits and vegetables.

Over time, Mom's highs got higher and her lows lower and longer. Weeks would sometimes pass and we wouldn't see her at all. Our food would run low. Janelle dropped out of school at sixteen to get a job. She pays most of our rent now, too, and makes sure we have food at all times. Eggs and milk. Pasta. I try to help out in the ways I can by cleaning and cooking meals. But Janelle refuses to let me leave school and get a full-time job, no matter what. I know she only stays in this shithole so I'm not alone.

Janelle insists that she didn't need school to be a famous hair stylist, but I know how much she sacrificed for me. One day, I'm going to make sure I make enough money for the two of us to get out of here. I'm not letting anything or anyone stop me. I just have to survive long enough to make it out.

JESSICA RUBEN

CHAPTER 3

J anelle and I walk underground and get on the six train, heading uptown. Quickly finding two empty seats next to each other, we drop down before anyone else can grab them. Janelle lets out a loud breath as we cross our legs, sitting in silence. I'm relieved Janelle isn't trying to talk, because I don't think I have it in me to speak right now. Just as the subway pulls into Fifty-Seventh Street, she stands up, holding the railing above us with one hand and telling me in a whisper and watery eyes that everything will be okay. She gets off, and I pull my bag closer to my chest, continuing my commute uptown to work.

I get to Angelo's Pawn, pulling out my key to open the old gray door. I glance up for a moment, noticing one of the electric-green lights on the signage is no longer on, turning the name of the shop into ANGELO'S PAN. As I push the door open, I make a mental note to remind Angelo to fix it. Getting inside, I immediately notice the frame of a man's silhouette behind the counter. My voice falls to my feet, my throat constricting. Carlos. He found me! Emptiness closes in with a threat of forcing me to pass out as my heart jumps from my chest.

Angelo turns around, and my knees threaten to buckle with relief. Shock lines his face while I feel myself begin to hyperventilate. My eyes know the man behind the counter isn't Carlos, but my body hasn't gotten the message yet. I know this is my Angelo, but all my body can understand is that a man is in front of me.

"Come on, doll. Relax." Angelo puts his thick arm around me and I immediately flinch, drawing back to get away from his touch. Stepping back, he brings me a chair and gently pushes me down to sit, telling me to put my head between my legs. When I finally feel calmer, I look up at him. He's in a clean button-down shirt and his dark hair is combed over to the side.

"Holy shit, sweetheart. But you've got some explaining to do." I inhale again and smell his cologne. The smell is sharp, but it's comforting. It's Angelo.

"Yeah, I know. I'm just—" I shake my head, feeling the tremors move through my body. I want to speak, but my throat tightens. I try to hold back my tears, but they refuse to be kept at bay. Part of me wants to let him take care of this issue for me so I never have to think of it again. But life doesn't work that way. The minute he gets the Borignone family involved, I'll just be one more girl they have control over. I'd be trading in one psychopath for another.

"Eve," he gets up and brings me a small bottle of water from the mini-fridge behind the counter. "Drink something and relax."

As the water streams down my throat, I finally calm down. I'm with Angelo. I'm safe here. In this moment, no one can hurt me.

"Tell me what's wrong."

"No, I...I...can't."

"Eve. I've known you long enough. I can't just sit here while you're like this. Tell me what's going on."

I look around the shop. It's small with an old carpeted floor and a large glass counter on the right side. It's filled with diamond rings and watches. I even see a new drum set and guitar in the corner along with a violin.

"That stuff is new?" I sniffle, pointing to the instruments. "It wasn't here last week."

"Yeah, doll. Stop deflecting. Now, talk to me."

"If I tell you, you need to swear to Christ that you won't do anything about it other than hear me out."

"Ah, you're bringing Jesus into this?" He raises his dark, bushy eyebrows.

"You know it," I reply with as much sass as I can muster.

"It must be some serious shit." I nod my head, tears dripping down my face. "All right." He lifts one hand as if under oath. "I swear." He nods solemnly. "Now talk."

I grip the bottom of the chair, feeling my knuckles burn as I open my mouth. I tell him about Carlos and the Snakes. By the time I'm finished, he's seething with anger.

"I'm gonna take care of that *fucker*!" He stands up, fury seeping through his pores.

"No! You can't! I don't want the mob after him. I can't get involved in that shit. And I can't owe anyone any favors. I can't do that—"

"Eve. That motherfucker is going to come back for you." He points to me. "I've heard of Carlos. He's certifiable."

"No," I tell him forcefully. "Janelle has friends. She's going to ask someone to talk to Carlos—"

"Christ, Eve. Are you kidding me? The Snakes are trying to gain power on the streets. If he wants you, he isn't letting you go!"

"I have to do this my way. I'll never forgive you if you tell Antonio. And how do we even know he took what happened seriously? I was in the wrong place at the wrong time. Maybe…maybe Carlos forgot about me already."

He blinks at me, giving a no-nonsense stare. He knows I'm not going to budge.

"Just remember, Antonio can probably have someone burned alive in the middle of Times Square without the cops saying a word. I want you to know that getting the family involved is always an option. It's the best option. Hell, they'll make sure he disappears—"

"Well, it can't be an option for me." I shake my head. "No way."

He stands up, pacing the room. Finally, he stops and turns to me. "It's time to teach you to shoot. You don't want to get the family involved, fine. But I'm not letting you walk around unarmed."

I stare at him shocked. "A…gun?" My nerves start up, but I swallow them down. "Angelo, I can't have a gun. Is it even legal?"

He rolls his eyes and starts to laugh. "Ah, my little Eve. I should nickname you *Double E* for Eve Esquire. You better be my lawyer someday, if—God forbid—I ever need one." He laughs at me as I blow my nose with a tissue from the counter.

I've got to give it to him; Angelo is making a lot of sense right now. I really do need some protection. This way, I won't have to lean on anyone else. "I guess it's self-defense, right?"

"You got it." He winks. "Self-defense."

I nod my head. "Okay. Teach me." My voice is full of false bravado. I can do this.

We walk together out of the shop, the door automatically locking with a *click* behind us. Ten minutes later, we enter an old rundown building. Getting down into the basement level, he opens a fireproof door to another set of steps.

Angelo flicks on the lights and my eyes widen in surprise. It's a completely new and modern space, totally at odds with the rest of the building. I've heard about these underground bunker spaces, but never could have imagined this! He walks me over to a glass cabinet with rows of rifles and guns. Choosing a small handgun from the first row, he pulls it out and brings it with us to a table in the back of the room.

"Where the hell are we, Angelo?" I look around nervously.

"Don't ask questions you don't want the answers to, doll." He gently places a hand on my shoulder. "Just stay with me and focus." He sits down, gesturing with his hand for me to sit beside him.

"Now Eve, this is a nine-millimeter pistol." He lifts up the gun. "Some people call it a Glock." I suck in a sharp inhale of air, scared. "Don't be afraid." He puts the gun down and touches my hand; I swallow the excess saliva building in my mouth. Opening a drawer, he pulls out some bullets. Picking up the gun, he demonstrates.

"You see this button here?" He points. "You press it to eject the magazine. Make sure to insert the ammunition one at a time into the top with the round side toward you until the magazine is full. Then put the magazine back in and up until you hear this click. Now it's locked." I nod my head.

"Before you shoot, you got to make sure the safety is disengaged. Then take your palm like this, and pull the slide to the back and then release it. Now your gun is ready." I watch him carefully, trying to memorize the steps.

He has me go through the motions upward of twenty times until I finally start to feel comfortable holding and loading.

"Good job." He praises me, as I smile happily. "Now, it's time for the fun part." He winks, handing me a set of earplugs and headphones. "Wearing both will protect your ears better." He walks me to the other end of the shop where I see a target made of paper. It's a black circle on a white background.

I put in the earplugs and slide on my headphones, pulling my hair back into a tight ponytail. The rest of my afternoon is spent learning how to shoot the gun. Once I get the hang of it, I don't want to stop.

"Can we come back?" I scream, forgetting my ears are totally plugged up. I see, but can't hear him laughing. Finally, I pull everything out of my ears and repeat myself, in a normal voice. He responds with more laughter, shaking his head.

"Yeah, we can, sweetheart. Anytime." He winks and throws a large arm around my shoulders. My heart fills.

We walk back upstairs and finally leave the building. "It's always the little ones like you who manage to be the best shots." His grin has pride written all over it.

We walk back into the pawnshop together, my purse much heavier. I must admit, I feel a hell of a lot safer now. Stronger, even. My life is my own to protect. If any of those thugs try to get me—

"Eve?" Angelo says, shaking me out of my thoughts.

"Yeah?" I turn to him expectantly.

"College, all right? You're too good for this shit. I want more for you. Better."

"I know." I nod. "I'm meeting Ms. Levine tomorrow night at her apartment. She's gonna help me fill out my applications. Deadline is next month, and I gotta get a move on."

"That's my girl."

VINCENT & EVE | RISING

CHAPTER 4

It's eight o'clock on Friday night, and my mom just left for work. I'm hanging out on the couch freshly showered, my wet hair wrapped up in a towel, turban-style.

Other than going to school and back during the week, and Angelo's on the weekends—I've basically been stuck inside my apartment, panicked that Carlos will find me. It's been two weeks since the incident.

Janelle asked someone to speak to him, and apparently, he said he'd leave me alone for a while. But what does *a while* even mean? I gulp, trying to push all thoughts of Carlos from my head. On a positive note, I've been reading up a storm. Janelle always tells me I can't live in a fictional world. Well, I'd beg to differ. I've moved from one book to the next so quickly that characters have been getting jumbled up in my head. But, I'd rather that than the alternative of thinking about my own situation.

"Should we order Dominos? They've got some kick-ass coupons going on right now," Janelle shouts from the kitchen. I look over to see her head stuck inside the refrigerator, probably pushing leftovers around. I've been cooking us food all week, and I know we have some good things in there. But a hot slice of pizza sounds amazing right now.

"Yeah. Let's do it. Can you make sure to get one of those ranch dipping cups on the side with the cheesy bread?"

She closes the fridge, smiles right at me. "Hell, yes we can!" I laugh as we hear Juan from the apartment below scream at his mom about not wanting to take out the trash.

"For the love of all that is holy, that boy needs to grow up already and take out the garbage! The shoot is down the hall for God's sake!" Janelle's exasperation at Juan's antics cracks me up. Our building has a tendency to mirror a bad soap opera; we all can't help but weigh in on everyone's business. The walls being paper-thin doesn't help the situation, either. Unfortunately, I kissed Juan last year at an apartment party a few blocks over. He tried calling me a million times afterward, but I ignored him. When we bumped into each other in the stairwell a few weeks later, he glared at me like I killed his dog. Suffice it to say, we are no longer on friendly terms.

"Does he still hate you?" She chuckles.

"Ugh, yes. I just made out with him and I swear you'd think I took his virginity or something with the clinginess!" I throw my arms up in the air, exasperated.

"Speaking of virginity—" she starts with a smirk.

"—Oh, shut it, Janelle. Yes, we all know I'm an eighteen-year-old virgin, *blah blah blah.*" I roll my eyes.

"If you'd just stop wearing those baggy clothes and hiding yourself—"

"I'm not interested in that right now," I say, effectively cutting her off. "I wear these clothes to cover myself. I need to make sure I don't give any mixed signals to anyone."

She huffs in annoyance as she pulls out her hair and makeup tools. "I'm not going to pretend I like your look these days, because I don't. I'm doing your hair and makeup tonight. It's time to remind you that you're one hundred percent beautiful woman. I wish you'd find yourself a man," she sighs.

"I'm going to ignore you and just go with… yay, makeup!"

Janelle is brilliant in making people beautiful, but still, she has the worst taste in men. I watch as she rummages through her makeup box, gathering what she needs for me. I may not be a girly girl, but it feels good getting dolled up every once in a while, even if I won't be leaving the apartment.

She combs my hair and separates it into sections to blow-dry. I'm completely engrossed in a novel while she does some magic with a round hairbrush, turning my hair into what she calls *beach waves*. Who knows where she comes up with this hair terminology, but in the past few months, she's done my hair as *the leading lady,* which is straight and sleek*,* and *the rising star,* which are 1950s style ringlets. When my hair is done, she uses two butterfly clips to pull the front of my hair away from my face.

"Put that book down and look straight ahead." I do as she asks. Using her fingers, she smears cream all over my face. Tonight, she's testing out a makeup look called *the siren*. When she's finished, she hands me a little handheld mirror. I see black shadows with a hint of sparkle smoking around my large hazel eyes. My cheekbones look incredibly high, shaded with golden bronzer. *Wow*. Even I have to admit I look good right now.

"I'd normally do a red lip, but I want to go with a creamy nude instead. More Kim, you know?" I shrug. My sister and everyone else seems to be obsessed with Kardashian makeup.

"Since I let you do my hair and makeup—"

"Close your mouth while I line and fill your lips." I shut up while she gets within an inch of my face, squinting her eyes like I'd imagine a surgeon would do. My sister has zero shake in her hands. "Now press your lips together," she commands. As usual, I do as she says.

"Can I try on some of your clothes?" I lift my hands in prayer, trying to look sweet.

"Fine," she says grudgingly, grabbing a pack of Marlboro Lights from the coffee table. I wouldn't call Janelle a smoker per se, but she definitely enjoys a smoke or two when she wants to relax. I run into our room as quickly as I can before she changes her mind.

Drake's "Hotline Bling" blares from Juan's apartment; I can feel the floor shake from the bass. Janelle perches herself on the bedroom windowsill. Opening the window and lighting up her cigarette with her favorite black-and-silver Zippo, she blows rings of smoke into the night.

She sticks her head out the window. "Yo Juan, I love this song!" She's rolling her upper body to the beat of the music and lifting her hand in the air. He replies by turning the volume up.

Smiling, I raise my arms, dancing my way into her closet and letting the music filter through my body. Janelle and I have always loved to dance. I push my ass out and twerk Miley Cyrus style, my body undulating to the beat. Janelle lets out a "Whoop!" Her long blond hair waves down her back as she cheers for me to keep going. When the song changes, I finally stop and go through her section of our closet, deciding what to try first.

I'm in the midst of moving clothes around when she speaks up. "Have you finished all these books yet?" I turn to her as she points to the stack on my desk.

"I'm getting through them pretty quickly," I tell her, smiling as I pull the T-shirt off over my head. I look through my drawer and find a sexy lace bra I bought from Victoria's Secret earlier this year. I put it on before wearing one of Janelle's tops. I look in the mirror appreciatively; the shirt is caramel brown, cropped, and off the shoulder. The fabric is so soft against my olive skin. After putting on a pair of tight jeans, I stand on my tippy-toes, posing as if I were wearing a pair of high heels—with no one watching, I enjoy looking sexy. One day, I want to be able to dress how I please without being afraid.

Janelle lets out a slow whistle. "You look hot, Eve. Damn, girl!" I smile in a rare moment of confidence and she winks, singing along to another song on Juan's playlist. "God, I can't imagine what it'll be like for you one day in college. Do you think it'll be like *Gossip Girl*? All those rich kids, having nothing to worry about other than their clothes and boyfriends?"

"Yeah. I don't know. Maybe? I'm going to do the best I can though, and that's IF I get in…" I let out a long sigh. There's no sense in getting crazy about colleges when I may not even get accepted, or get enough money in scholarships and grants to be able to go.

She crosses her heavy black boots in front of her, a stark contrast to the flowery minidress she's wearing. Her phone rings and she answers it. "Yo—wait, what? No shit! Look, I gotta go." Hanging up the phone, a smile rushes across her face.

"Hey, little sister. Guess what?" She says in a singsong voice.

I turn my head to her, raising my eyebrows in question.

"Carlos is in jail right now!" She is ecstatic.

"What?" I exclaim, my heart skipping a beat.

"You heard me. That was Vania calling. She heard from Juaquin that Carlos went to jail after a drug deal gone wrong. Some undercover cop bought from him yesterday in the park!" She leans her head out the window screaming, "Louder, Juan!" She laughs out loud.

I feel my eyes widen as the music turns up. "Maybe that means they'll lay low for a while, right? How long will he be gone for?" With a voice full of hope, I watch as Janelle fist-pumps into the air.

"Who knows? All I care about is the fact that tonight, he's fuckin' gone! Wait, we have to celebrate!" All at once, her face changes to mischief. "You know what, Eve? It would be a waste for no one to see you looking this incredible. I know exactly where we're going." Her smile is contagious. She throws her lit cigarette out the window—and probably onto some unsuspecting pedestrian—and hops off the sill.

"Why can't you just put your cigarette in the ashtray? One of these days you're going to burn someone."

"I like to live dangerously, what can I say?" I roll my eyes at her, but we immediately start to laugh.

I want to tell her I'm still afraid to leave. What if one of Carlos's friends is out? "Look, Janelle—"

"You can't let that experience run your life, Eve. I don't want your fear to rob you of your life! Carlos is off the street for now. We're going out tonight! You. Me. *Out.*" She punctuates her words, making sure I understand we're leaving.

"I'm not taking *no* for an answer. We may have to live in the Blue Houses, but we have to make it work. You're eighteen years old for God's sake; you gotta try to act normal."

I shake out my shoulders. I need to do this. Janelle is right. How long do I intend to never leave home at night? She's with me and has my back; it's not as if I'll be alone. I can do this. No, I NEED to do this. Carlos is gone. I can bring my gun. I'll be just fine.

The doorbell rings and she claps her hands. "Perfect timing! First pizza, then we're outta here!"

She pays the delivery guy in cash while I fill our glasses with water from the sink. Sitting down at our kitchen table, we open up the box with the steaming pie and smile at each other. When we're done, Janelle jumps up and heads into our bedroom. I can imagine her rummaging through our small coat rack in the corner of the room for her bag. She walks out with our purses in hand and a pair of high-heeled pumps for me.

"Girl, why is your bag so damn heavy?" She hands me mine and I dart my eyes to the side. I haven't told her yet about my gun. I know I should, but I'm not sure what her reaction will be. And right now, I just want to enjoy the night.

"Where are we going?" I ask, hoping my subject change will work.

"You'll see," she tells me, eyes twinkling. Pulling out a tube of lip gloss from her bag, she applies hers, adding a second coat to mine.

She leads me out of our tiny apartment, practically pushing me through the door. I'm wearing her clothes, face full of makeup, dark hair in long waves down my back. Her hand holds mine and she squeezes it three times. I'm afraid, but I know I can always trust her promises. With Janelle by my side, I'm safe.

Once we walk over the threshold of our apartment, I can't wipe the smile off my face. The combination of surprise and excitement to be out with Janelle is dizzying. I follow her down the concrete steps. We're both so sublimely happy about Carlos being behind bars, we're practically floating down the stairwell.

"Hi George!" we say, stepping over our drunken third-floor neighbor. His clothes are full of holes and his hair is matted on his head. Even though he's sprawled on the bottom of the steps, he's still gripping his beer bottle like his life depends on it. Janelle and I know him, though, and he's harmless.

"Looking good girls," he slurs, a sloppy smile on his face. Janelle continues to walk, but I pause to open my wallet and hand him some loose change.

"God bless you, Eve. Take care of yourself, my sweet girl." I nod to him and smile, running down the remainder of the steps to catch up with Janelle.

We get on the crosstown bus just as it pulls into the front of our building, taking a window seat in the back. Within twenty-minutes, we're in the trendy Meatpacking District on West Fourteenth Street. While it used to be full of slaughterhouses and packing plants, it's now one of the swankiest areas of the city.

"Your eyes look amazing," Janelle tells me, angling her body toward mine.

"Yeah, it's cool."

"At this rate, I'll be traveling with Beyoncé doing her hair on her next European tour. By the way, she definitely used a surrogate this time around and faked her pregnancy."

"Totally!" I exclaim. We laugh as she does a little shimmy in her seat.

Smiling confidently, she brings her hands to my hairline. Taking the small clips out from the front of my hair, she uses the tips of her fingers to separate my dark waves, twirling them into an organized chaos.

She flips her long blond waves behind her. "You're growing up, angel baby," she says, using a nickname she gave me when we were kids. "You gonna try to catch yourself some rich guy in college? Seriously, you're looking stunning tonight. My baby sister is a goddess."

I drop my head for a second, embarrassed by her compliment. "Don't be crazy, Janelle. If I go there, it will be for one thing: grades." I turn my head back toward the window, ending the conversation before it can begin. I have a single-track mind right now, and I won't allow a guy to derail my plans. It's not as if any guy has ever excited me, anyway.

I look down at my tight jeans and cropped shirt. I know I don't look overly sexual, but I'm not used to looking like this out in public. Still, I don't want to let Janelle down. She put herself out to make me look good, and I want to show her that I'm not scared. I take a deep breath, letting the evening's excitement beat through my legs as I try to push all thoughts about my body and state of dress out of my mind. "So, what are we doing, anyway?" I finally ask.

"Are you sure you don't want to be surprised?" she asks me with a roguish grin.

"I mean, okay. Why not? I don't have to know everything beforehand." I let out a shaky smile and force a happy face, and Janelle laughs at me. We both know that I like preparing for everything. Surprises don't really go with my personality. Her gaze travels down to my chest and her smile turns to full blown.

Janelle shakes her head at me. "Oh come on Eve, don't be afraid of having huge knockers. I can't wait to buy a pair that look like yours one day." My face turns crimson, but it only makes her laugh harder.

"Oh, this is our stop!" Janelle jumps out of the seat and grabs her bag as she walks to the front of the bus. I follow her out. As I take a few steps, I notice my top riding up, showing a sliver of stomach. I pull it down only to realize I'm revealing more of my cleavage. I decide I'd rather show a little tummy than have my boobs pop out. I pull my blouse back up, again. *Shit!*

"Stop fussing with your top, Je-sus," she says in her exaggerated way, as she starts down the sidewalk.

Walking on the cobblestone isn't easy in these shoes, but I do my best not to face plant. I want to slow down so I can people watch, but there is no stopping Janelle. She's on a mission to get wherever we're going, incessantly checking her phone. We continue to speed-walk a few blocks, finally stopping in front of a large abandoned warehouse. A huge man with a military buzz cut, looking angry as hell, stands guard at the front door. There are a few people hanging around, casually smoking and checking us out. Janelle ignores them, walking straight to the big guy.

"Hey Lenny," my sister says flirtatiously. He looks us both up and down and opens the door with a grunt, letting us inside without a word.

CHAPTER 5

We walk down a set of narrow steps to a basement. I'd be scared if it weren't for all the loud hardcore hip-hop I hear below me. I pause when the room comes into view; the place is teeming with people. A large Lucite bar circles the room's perimeter and lounge furniture is arranged in clusters close to the bar area. But in the center of the room, what looks like over a hundred people are standing together. I furrow my eyebrows, confused. What are they doing there?

"Yo, Eve. Hurry!" My sister waves to me from the bottom of the steps, and I run down to reach her. When I'm safely by her side, she grabs my hand and squeezes. Janelle's got me.

We move forward into the pack, inserting ourselves into the crowd. She pushes bodies aside with her shoulder while I squeeze through behind her, sliding myself into the space she clears. It's humid, and everyone seems to be glistening with sweat. Most of the girls we pass are wearing what I'd guess is typical club attire: slutty, sexy, and easily removable.

We pass by a huge guy who is standing up on a chair; he's yelling out sums to someone below while taking fistfuls of cash from people. The excitement is tangible. I hold Janelle's hand tightly, not knowing what the hell is going on, but eager to find out.

"That's Leo, in the white polo shirt!" Janelle yells, turning her face to mine. "Don't let go of me, okay?" She winks and turns forward again, moving more aggressively through the throngs. I duck my head, trying to avoid getting elbowed in the face. The rap music gets louder as we cut deeper into the crowd; it's the Rough Ryders' Anthem, "Stop, drop, shut 'em down, open up shop..."

I can finally spot the white Polo, but Leo's facing away from us. He looks as if he's talking with a group of friends, his arm around a girl. He seems really clean-cut from behind, and I'm wondering how my sister is with a guy who looks so *preppy*. After everything I've heard about him, this isn't what I was expecting at all. But when he turns around to us, I see the black gauges in both his ears and a silver barbell through his lower lip; tattoos in an array of colors peek out from under his sleeves. Ah, now that's more Janelle's style. I internally roll my eyes at the asshole who treats my sister like shit.

"What the FUCK, Leo?" Janelle screams, her arm shooting out in front of her as she tries to take a swing at the girl—a cheaper-looking version of Janelle, if I'm being honest. He quickly removes his arm and brings it around Janelle's shoulders, stopping her from doing any damage. Leaning down and smelling the top of her hair, he ignores her outburst like it's the most normal thing in the world. I watch as he winks at one of his friends as if he's got everything under control.

He turns to Janelle. "Just stay by me. Things are gonna get a lot crazier once it starts." Janelle stares the other girl down, and she quickly scurries away.

I stare at Leo, acne scars marring his cheekbones. He isn't conventionally good-looking, but his confidence makes him attractive. I inhale sharply, noticing his eyes are full of anticipation and tinged with frenzy. Unfortunately, I know that look all too well. He's obviously on something, and I silently curse Janelle. I've said it a million times already, but she can do so much better.

Moving my gaze away from them, I realize we're standing in a circle and the center is empty. Before I can ask Janelle what's happening, she grabs Leo around the waist and tilts her head up to kiss him. I watch as her tongue enters his mouth. She moans when he grips her scalp, bringing their bodies together. Trying to ignore the sinking feeling that I'll end up as a third wheel tonight, I busy myself by fussing with my hair and checking my phone. I'm used to being Janelle's silent shadow out in public, but tonight, I was hoping for more.

It's so hot in here that my hair is already starting to frizz from the humidity. I rummage through my bag for a clip. Finding one, I twist my hair up off my neck.

Leo finally pulls back from Janelle and I turn to him just as he takes a pill out of his pocket. "Here you go." He smiles. She seductively opens her mouth as he drops the pill onto her tongue. She shuts her mouth, swallowing it with no water. When she licks her lips, I let out a sigh, wishing she wouldn't do that in front of me.

Sensing me watching, she turns to Leo. "Don't be a jackass, honey. Say *hi* to my baby sister, Eve." Her voice is breathy; she keeps her arms wrapped around his middle, looking up at him like he's the greatest man alive.

He looks at me slyly, checking me out from my toes up to my eyes. "Hey, Eve. Nice to meet you." I turn red from his blatant ogling.

The sound of a foghorn has me turning toward the center of the circle. "Ladies and gentlemen, welcome to the Fight Zone!" A man in the center of the ring shouts. He looks like he's in his mid-forties, but has obviously been banged up a time or two. His nose is crooked from what looks like multiple breaks, and he struts with a limp. Regardless, he's all confidence. Moving around the center of the circle, he seems to be enjoying all eyes on him. For a moment, people's voices quiet down.

"First," he pauses, clearing his throat. "We've got the undefeated Jack 'the Ripper' McDougal, versus Michael 'Mayhem' Smith." The noise level returns to deafening. I look around at the crazed faces of the spectators. Entering the circle is a guy who looks like he eats girls like me between meals. He's shirtless, wearing only a pair of low-slung jersey shorts. As he bounces from one foot to the other, I cringe at his overblown muscles. The next guy appears from the other end of the room wearing a thin, white tank top. His hair is shaved into an electric-red Mohawk, and he's literally snarling at his opponent. My heart beats erratically as I look from side to side, realizing these guys don't even have gloves on! My mind is finally putting together the pieces of what I'm about to witness. Something that feels a lot like dread pools in my stomach. I'm about to watch an illegal cage fight.

"The rules are simple," the announcer tells the fighters. "Don't kick each other in the balls. No biting or eye gouging. And for the fans..." He lifts his hands up, staring at us all. "Don't step into the circle, or risk becoming part of the maaaaadness!"

People begin to go berserk. I feel some spit fly onto me from someone standing near me and my body shudders. The fighters stand tall, glaring at each other. They're practically foaming at the mouth. The only thought repeating through my head is: *HOLY SHIT!*

I turn my head left and right, my stomach cramping; I'm in the front row. There is no way I can move as the crowd is totally closed in behind me. I see people across the circle with their hands up, fists pumping in the air. They're waiting for blood, and from the looks of these two fighters, the blood will definitely be flowing.

I turn to Janelle, grabbing her shoulders. "We're too close to the front!" I yell, staring up into her eyes. I'm willing her to snap out of her drug-induced trance. Unfortunately for me, her eyes have already dilated. She leans down and puts her sweaty forehead on mine, her smile so big I think it might split her face.

She throws an arm around my neck. "Don't worry baby girl, this will be amazing! God, I love you so much!" She squeezes me close to her. Letting me go, she takes a huge gulp of water from a plastic bottle and continues shouting along with the crowd. I try to stand on my tip-toes to get a better look at my surroundings. Is there an empty space I can run through?

Unfortunately, the entire circle is shut tight with bodies. When I realize there's no way out, I close my eyes and count down from twenty. Before I open them, I inhale deeply through my nose, trying to find a modicum of calm. *I'm going to be okay.* When I open my eyes, I feel like the wind has been knocked out of me. Right across from me is the most attractive man I've ever laid eyes on.

He's a head above the rest, black hair that's longer at the top and shorter at the sides; it's a little wild, but incredibly sexy. I have never seen anyone who looks quite like him. The entire fight scene ahead of me seems to come to a standstill as I study him, the breath catching in my throat. I hear screaming all around me, but it may as well be on mute.

I watch as he pushes his hair back and casually throws an arm around a redhead. She's tall and thin, with wide blue eyes and thick auburn hair, mirroring a model in a Neutrogena skin commercial. Laughing at something he says, it's clear she fits the mold of an all-American beauty.

Turning back to him, I take in every single move he makes. Holy shit, he's gorgeous. I hear Janelle cheering wildly next to me, but the shrill sound barely registers.

He has something I can't put my finger on. Maybe it's the slight slant in his eyes or his razor-cut cheekbones and chiseled square jaw. It's just a trace of something unique, and it doesn't make him look kind. In fact, his face and entire demeanor is absolutely feral.

He whispers something into the girl's ear. I wonder what he's telling her. She bites her lower lip as she listens to him, and in that moment, I wish it were me in her spot. For the first time in my life, I'm practically vibrating with awareness over a man. Just then, he decides to raise his head. He glances around, seemingly looking for someone. His eyes immediately pause at mine, catching my stare. I've been caught! My heart stutters; I'm a deer in head-lights as embarrassment runs through me.

Strangely, he isn't staring at me like a weirdo. Instead, his eyes seem to see straight into my soul; it's unnerving, but in some unexpected way, feels *right*. I open my eyes a little wider, feeling my lips part. He squints as a smile spreads across his full lips, settling into his eyes. I can't help the flush rising through my body.

We continue to watch each other, and it feels as if energy is passing be-tween us. He pushes his hair back again, and I see the wide expanse of his chest. I try not to swoon from the visual. I see boys all the time, but none of them make me feel like *this*. Who am I kidding? None of them are as hot as this man in front of me. I see him chuckle as he notices my eyes widening; is he laughing at me? Of course he is. He knows how good-looking he is and what he's doing.

Then, I do what any girl would do in my situation. I turn behind me to make sure that he isn't actually having a conversation with someone else. But when I turn back to him, I see his head is thrown backward as if he's laughing out loud. I feel like an utter dork when he waves back at me and mouths the word, "Hello." Just watching his lips move is enough to make my pulse errat-ic. I'm embarrassed, but burning up from our wordless banter.

Surprising myself, I give him the finger with a smile—because, well, the asshole is laughing at me! The physical distance between us, combined with the fact that he is a stranger, makes me brave. I mean, he doesn't know me from a hole in the wall. Chances are, after this weird little flirting thing we've got going on, I won't be seeing him again. I may as well enjoy this moment. He raises his eyebrows as if me giving him the finger is cute. I watch as his eyes squint and lips turn up, transforming his face into something breathtak-ing.

I take my hair out of the clip and shake it loose with my fingertips, giving myself a break from our eye contact while attempting to channel sexy. When I glance back up at him, his eyes widen. Now it's my turn to smile. He likes what he sees, and it both scares and thrills me.

Another blast of the foghorn, signaling the end of the fight. I flinch from the sound, immediately brought back into the center of the ring. "The Ripper wins with one hundred thirty strikes!" the announcer yells into the crowd, while some people cheer and others boo.

The announcer continues, his loud voice ratcheting up even higher. "I think it's time to bring out our main attraction here tonight. This guy coming is one crazy motherfucker. I'm beginning to ask myself if there is anyone out there who can beat him. There's some talk that the UFC has been asking the same thing. But who knows, maybe the Ripper will finally take him down, what do you all think?" His face flashes crimson from the exertion of his yelling. "Are you all ready for... the Bull?" He's chuckling like a devil, and the crowd is eating it up.

People jump up and down. "Holy shit," I say out loud, the mob turning into a mosh pit. They chant: "Bull...Bull...Bull." I turn to my sister in confusion as the music changes from gangster rap to heavy metal. Janelle bounces on her toes with excitement. Leo yells with what looks like a combination of bloodlust and eagerness, while the entire crowd shrieks. I don't know what's going on, but I find myself waiting with nervous tension as to what's to come. Whoever he is, he's obviously a big deal.

I turn my head up to search for the guy I've been staring at only to realize that he is no longer in his spot. I scan the circle, frustrated that he disappeared. My eyes leap from face to face, the sounds of the crowd fading into the back of my mind when I see a large figure sauntering in the center of the ring. My eyes immediately expand—it's him. I can't take my eyes off him as he strips off his shirt, and apparently, neither can anyone else. His body is perfectly cut. He's huge, with rippling abs and thick, muscular arms. My insides liquefy.

He stands in the center of the ring, jumping up and down to get his blood flowing. The Ripper rolls his beefed-up shoulders, stretching out his thick neck from side to side. They appear evenly matched in height, both well over six feet. The Ripper looks as if he juices for breakfast. All of the signs of steroid use are obvious; his traps are gigantic and covered with severe acne. Meanwhile, the Bull smirks with confidence, shuffling his feet. I let myself ogle his physique. A perfectly cut V of muscle leads down into his shorts. My mouth runs dry, imagining what must be below. I flush as dirty thoughts of him race through my head.

People continue to yell as the fight begins, but my eyes are glued to the Bull in the center of the ring.

The Ripper lifts his leg in the air for a kick, but the Bull steps back easily, dodging any connection and getting the crowd crazed. He's barely breaking a sweat while the Ripper pants. The Bull is playing a game for the crowd, dancing around the circle with a cocky smile while the Ripper tries over and over again to make contact. The Bull's movements are so agile, almost logic-defying for a man so huge. The Ripper looks at the Bull with fury, bearing his teeth like a rabid animal. Finally, the Bull gives the crowd what they're begging for as he steps closer to his opponent, throwing punches into the Ripper's face. I wince, watching blood stream from the Ripper's nose down into his mouth. The Bull steps back and turns his body in a different stance while the Ripper shakes his head back into reality. Just as he seemingly wakes up, the Bull throws a wide kick directly into the Ripper's face, the force bringing his enormous body down to the ground. The crowd lets out a collective "ooo-hhhh" as the Ripper drops like a dead weight.

Before the Ripper can even try to stand, the Bull drops down and strad-dles him. He's slamming his fists into the Ripper's face like a beast, going at him like a man in it for the kill. The Ripper is trying to claw himself free, thrashing his arms and legs in wild directions, but the Bull has him secured in some sort of technical-looking hold. There's no way the Ripper is getting out of this.

I hear an animalistic grunt and silence ensues as the Bull stops his move-ments. Sweat pours down his face as he pants, rising up. People are waiting impatiently, peering into the circle. Will the Ripper stand? The music con-tinues to blare and all eyes are focused on the floor, where the Ripper, now bloody, turns to his side and groans. When it's clear he isn't able to get up on his own, the crowd starts screaming again. The announcer grabs the Bull's hand, raising it up in the air as a dark and threatening smile spreads across the Bull's face.

Beads of perspiration roll down the Bull's chest, and I swallow hard, cat-aloging it as one of the sexiest things I've ever seen in my life. Some friends of the Ripper come into the ring's center, lifting him up and dragging him off to the side. Turning my gaze back to the Bull, I find him staring straight at me. After what I just saw, I should be running for the hills. Instead, I give him a megawatt smile that I couldn't stop even if I tried. Suddenly, the crowd swallows him, and just like that, he's gone.

I turn to my sister with a happiness on my face that rivals her drug-induced glee. People are dispersing, frenzied hands exchanging money. I feel a wave of nervousness that I've lost him. My eyes scan the area, but at five-foot-one, it's impossible for me to get a good view of anything other than people's chests. An irrational panic hits me as I wonder if I'll ever see him again. I grab Janelle's hand like a lifeline, wanting her to tell me about this guy. "Who was that?" I ask.

"Oh my God. I mean—*look* at him. Have you ever seen someone so fuck-hot? He's dangerous as hell, which adds to the hot factor by like, ten billion. He's super shady though. No one knows his real name." All I can do is shake my head in wonder. Because the truth is, never in my life have I seen a man who affected me like that. And it isn't merely the fact that he's so physically striking. It's more. At least, it felt like more.

Before Janelle can start talking, the crowd shifts toward the bar, sweeping us into its clutches. Leo possessively drapes an arm around Janelle. It's clear from the smile on his face that he's thrilled to have made some cash tonight. Janelle says hi to random people as we pass; I shouldn't be surprised she's a regular in this scene. I know she keeps this side of her life to herself; she's always trying to shelter me.

I continue searching for the Bull as we walk, but the lights have dimmed, making it even harder to see anyone.

We get to the bar and Leo manages to order a few quick drinks from the bartender, which he immediately hands to us. "Thanks, Leo," I say, sipping it slowly. As the liquid makes contact with my tongue, I'm jolted by how disgusting it tastes. I swallow it down painfully, trying not to spit it out. Janelle smiles at me knowingly.

She bends down to whisper in my ear. "Be careful, okay? Drink a cup of water for every alcoholic drink you have. Never forget that." She presses her warm lips on my forehead and I smile.

I look down in my cup, noticing it's already half empty; surprisingly, it doesn't taste so bad anymore. I'm glad I have it in my hands. It gives me something to hold while I glance around, trying to find the Bull.

I finally spot him hanging out with a group of people by some couches, close to a corridor. I want to scream with excitement, but keep myself calm. Looking closely, it seems as if everyone in his group is angled toward him. They're chatting away while he leans against a wall, relaxed and utterly sexy.

The people he's standing with are different from the rest of the crowd. They give off an air of money and entitlement. Unlike everyone I know who lives life trying to prove their worth with attitude and bravado, this group just has an innate confidence. They stand straight like they have a right to be here, owning their lives and their bodies without any fear. Is it just a matter of them having money? Or maybe their schooling? Or maybe it's as simple as the way they were raised—taught to believe that they're valuable.

I don't want my poor life; I want more. I want THAT. I bow my head and close my eyes for a moment, swearing to myself if I can get into college, I'm going to focus. I don't want to mess it up. *God, please don't let me mess it up.* I don't want to live this life anymore. I want to succeed. I take another sip of my drink, my vision refocusing on the Bull.

The girls around him wear stiletto heels with beautiful red soles peeking out from the arches. That redhead he had his arm around before is still next to him, model-perfect in a simple dark shirt and low-rise jeans. She's wearing a leather jacket with silver studs along the collar that, from the looks of it, probably costs more than I'll make for an entire summer at the pawnshop.

Rubbing his arm while he's staring out into the room, he turns as people come to chat him up.

Unlike the others who are dressed expensively, he is super casual in black sweatpants and a black T-shirt. The muscle definition in his chest and arms can be seen from where I'm standing, and it has me breathing heavy.

My whole life, I've never asked for anything. Nothing has truly ever belonged to me. But for the first time, I see something I want. My instinct is to feel unworthy. Why should I need or want someone like him? I'm not fancy or rich. I don't even have any control over my life or—as Carlos showed me—my body. The reality is that I could be heading home tonight and get shot for being in the wrong place at the wrong time. Hell, Carlos could get out of jail, find me again, and decide he's going to do whatever he pleases with me. Maybe what I need to take from all of this is that I've only got one life to live; I need to try to enjoy it.

People step in front of him, blocking my view again. I want to scream at them to move. I may never be able to have him, but I want to at least look and dream. The way he stared at me earlier made me feel alive and beautiful, and right now, I'd do almost anything to be seen that way again. He steps away from the wall and begins walking away from his group, toward the bar. The bar. *I'm* near the bar! My heart thumps wildly in my chest, and I'm not sure what I'm supposed to do: run, stay still, turn away?

As he walks forward, people jump in front of him, wanting to shake his hand or say hello. He's cordial, making small talk with a few guys but not stopping for more than a moment or two. I can't take my eyes off him, but I'm also terrified of him seeing me. When I know he's getting close, my body makes the choice for me. I do an about-face, turning away. I simply can't let him see me. I realize how absurd this is, and childish, for that matter. But I just...can't.

I turn myself toward the bar so I can at least watch him from my side eye. Janelle stops him, trying to get his attention. I tune into her voice and freeze. "Hey Bull, great fight tonight." Her voice is higher pitched than usual.

I can only imagine what he must be thinking. My throat burns as I anticipate him wanting her. She's so beautiful and experienced and knows men in a way that I never have. My chest hurts with the realization that a man like him would always rather be with a woman like her. I slowly turn my head, trying to see if anything is happening between them. They're chatting, and her body language is spelling out her attraction. I see her giggle and place a hand on his chest. I can't see whether or not he's enjoying the attention. I want to turn around and yell: "No! I want that one. Let me have just that one, and you can take anyone else in this entire place!" My mind finally shuts up as I watch him remove her fingers from his body. I'd be lying if I said I didn't feel relief at his dismissal of her.

At the bar, he raises an arm to get the bartender's attention. I'm sweating with nerves. There are only a few people between him and me. Am I going to just let this go? I want to turn to him, but still can't manage it; my feet feel as if they're nailed to the floor. I know he's ordering his drink when I see the elation on the bartender's face—her reaction to him annoying but understandable. She bends forward, showing off her huge boobs.

I cringe, rolling my eyes at her blatant display. "Come on Eve," I say quietly to myself. "Get a grip and turn the hell around! You can do this, girl!" All at once, I get sick of myself. I'm tired of melting into the background, letting everyone make choices for me. The mental pep talk works as I steel my spine and pivot, straightening my body so I'm facing him. His eyes are trained forward. God, he's huge. Even bigger up close. If I were in a cartoon, my mouth would be watering.

Glancing around the room while he waits for his drink, our eyes connect. Recognition passes through his features as I stare, trying not to seem too eager. He smiles as if we've known each other for ages, lifting his hand to me.

After taking his drink from the bartender, he drops some cash down and moves over to where I'm standing. I move to take a huge gulp of my drink, willing it to give my mouth words. He leans in toward me as I press my lips to the rim.

"Having fun?" His voice is penetrating, and my knees weaken from the deep sound.

I force my head to look up at him as I try to revive my brain. I wish I had something good to say. Unfortunately, all I can come up with is, "Yeah, I'm cool." I nod my head and bring my drink back to my lips, taking another deep swallow. Now that I'm faced with him, all the flirtation I managed while he was physically far from me has turned to dust.

He moves closer and I'm immediately assaulted by how good he smells. It's fresh laundry, mint, sweat—and something else I can't put my finger on. Holy shit, but if I could bottle his scent, I'd be a millionaire right now. He lifts his muscular arm, taking a deep pull from his beer. I'm having a visceral reaction to him and there is no stopping it.

"I'm Vincent," he says, giving me his huge hand. I stare up at him through my long lashes, placing my hand in his. I barely reach the center of his torso.

"I'm Eve," I stare up, trying to sound self-assured. His hand still surrounds mine; the contact short-circuits my brain.

"Why do you look so mad all of a sudden, Eve? Did I do something?" He smirks, licking the corner of his full lips. I get the feeling he's toying with me. He must know that I'm way out of my depth—under the ocean and drowning in heat.

I answer him, hoping to salvage the conversation without acting like a complete moron. "No, of course not. I guess I'm just a little tipsy?" I let out a little laugh and shrug, willing my voice not to squeak. He threads his fingers through mine intimately and for whatever reason, I feel secure.

"Nah. You look good to me," he smiles. "Can I get you another drink? Yours is about done." He glances down into my cup, raising his eyebrows as if to say, *"See, it's empty."*

"Oh, um, I should probably just have water now," I reply shyly, remembering Janelle's tip about drinking water. He looks at me with furrowed brows and I immediately wonder if I said the wrong thing. Should I have said *yes*? Shit!

He nods his head, understanding that I'm not trying to get drunk. Little does he know that this small drink went straight into my virgin bloodstream faster than one of his punches to the Ripper's face.

We meander back to the bar, my hand still entwined with his.

"Do you come to these fights often?" He puts his drink down at the bar, using his free hand to wave the bartender back again. Before I can answer him, she's back in front of us, ignoring the other people who have been waiting.

"Hello again, handsome. Ready for another?" She tilts her head to the side flirtatiously, clearly attention seeking.

"Thanks." His voice is disinterested.

She purses her lips seductively, not willing to give up too quickly. "You gonna give me your real name one of these nights, Bull?"

He chuckles. "Just two cups of water, please." He gives her a panty-dropping grin that has her squirming. She moves to get the waters when I realize that I actually know his name. Vincent. My heart flutters that he's given something to me that he hasn't given to the sexy bartender.

After bringing the water, Vincent hands one to me first and picks up the second for himself. I watch his Adam's apple bob as he swallows his entire glass without a breath. I try to drink mine the same way, but end up choking. He starts to laugh at me and I roll my eyes. "I'm trying here!" I tell him, embarrassed.

"Damn, you're sweet." His eyes sparkle and my heart thumps.

Picking up his beer from the bar, he leads me over to where his friends are standing. The music blares as throngs of people walk down the steps.

"The place is packed." I feel my anxiety rise as strangers move against me. My heart pounds; I still can't handle being touched. Immediately noticing my discomfort, he backs us toward a wall and stands in front of me, not letting anyone other than him get in my space. I should be scared, but for whatever reason, his presence makes me feel secure.

"Yeah, it's definitely full tonight." He turns his head, looking around the room. "The deejay is a friend of mine and he's pretty good. Brings in a decent crowd." He takes another swallow of his beer as I nod my head, trying to act cool. Meanwhile, I'm anything but.

"So, you like what you saw tonight?" His voice is inquisitive as he licks the corner of his lips again. I'm trying not to stare at his mouth, but I can't help myself. When I glance back into his eyes, he smiles at me knowingly. I flush, self-conscious that he keeps catching me.

Unsure what he wants to hear, I go with honesty. "No, underground fights aren't really my thing." I shift my weight from one foot to the other. I finally have the strength to look straight into his eyes and when I do, another connection passes between us like a zing.

"You aren't a regular."

All I can do is nod my head at his statement.

He looks around the room and takes my hand again, walking us to a lounge area that's roped off. The bouncer greets Vincent with a fist bump and lets us inside. "Sit. It'll be more comfortable for you here." I gingerly move to the edge of the couch, waiting for him to come next to me.

He sits, spreading his knees and leaning back against the cushions. "You know, these fights have picked up a lot of steam in the city." He casually drapes an arm around the back of the couch. "When I first started fighting at places like these, it was a small crowd and just for fun. But it's really turned into something." I watch as his eyes move from my eyes to my lips, then back up again.

"Well, aside from the obvious injury or death, the whole thing seems horribly stupid. What if one of these fighters has AIDS? I doubt anyone is getting tested and meanwhile blood is flying all over the place." Clearly, the alcohol has removed the filter from my brain and loosened my tongue. *Holy shit*. The look on his face is one of utter shock.

"Not that I'm saying you have AIDS—" I stutter, trying to backtrack.

His eyes open wider and he starts laughing, clapping his hands a few times as if I said the funniest thing he's ever heard. "Well, you have a point. But all fighters know what we're getting into when we sign up." He tilts his head to the side, daring me to keep going. Unfortunately, the side of my brain that no longer has a filter wants to rise up to his dare.

"Yeah, so do people when they're trying to score drugs. The state should know that this goes on and just admit it so they can regulate it. By turning a blind eye, they're letting people put their lives in danger." Apparently, my voice has been found, because I can't seem to shut the hell up!

He keeps chuckling. "And you think it's the job of New York to make sure I don't put my life in danger?" He smiles broadly.

"Of course I do. The health and safety of its citizens should be the number one priority of any government." I look him in the eye nervously, realizing that my rant may have just screwed this whole thing up. Turns out my brainiac alter ego is on full display tonight. One drink and it's unstoppable.

"Priority of the government, huh?" He lowers his head, getting close to my ear and whispers. "Well, the truth is I never go into a ring in this setting unless I know I'll pummel the guy. I've got a lot going on and can't risk getting hurt. I train like a monster too, so losing is really not possible. Most of these guys are untrained; beating them is a given."

His warm breath at my ear travels straight down into my core; I press my legs together. A guy drops down next to him and he moves his head away to chat.

Am I imagining all of this? I have an internal freak-out the size of a tornado going on in my brain. Thankfully, I have the mental capacity to text Janelle. I pull out my phone. I'm not sure if this is a one-way thing or if he's feeling it too. My lack of experience is rearing its ugly head.

ME: OH MY GODDDDDDDD I'm with the HOTTEST GUY EVER-RRR

JANELLE: Yay!!! Be safe but don't forget a thing, I want to hear all about this tomorrow

ME: He's so friggin' hot I can't see straight. I really can't. I need help!

JANELLE: Relax. You're gorgeous. BE HAPPY!!

…. Text me if you need me.

…. And taxi home, no late night bus! Nice out tonight—Blue Houses will be packed with people, so no worries!

ME: k.

JANELLE: I'm going to hang out at Leo's place for a while…;-)

I close my phone and drop it down in my bag. Part of me is scared as hell to be out all alone, but thoughts of the man next to me are keeping me afloat. A few guys have walked into our section and Vincent stands up to greet them. They're intimidating, all with slicked-back hair and suits. I stand up as Vincent grabs one of them in a friendly hug. "Eve, this is my boy, Tom." Vincent smiles.

As Tom starts talking about the fight, Vincent walks away. My brain screams, "What? No! Come back!" Tom takes a sip of his drink, not breaking eye contact with me. He seems nice enough, but I can feel his interest, and it's making me uncomfortable. I move my eyes away from him, trying to see where Vincent went. I hear Tom's voice, but none of what he actually says registers.

I turn back to him. "Huh? Sorry, my mind was on something else."

"The fights. Did you like em'?" He looks at me expectantly. He's tall, with sandy brown hair and light eyes. He's wearing a suit like the other guys. Actually, Vincent is the only casual one here.

"Did you all come from work or something?" I'm gesturing to his clothes and he starts to laugh. I immediately feel self-conscious, as if what I said was stupid.

"I guess you can call it that." He winks, taking a sip of his drink. I can easily imagine him driving to some college on the West Coast with his top down and girlfriend in the passenger seat of a Mercedes Benz.

He clears his throat.

"Yeah. The fights were cool. I've never seen anything like that before." I immediately realize how naïve I must have come across with my reply. I need a conversation redo.

He chuckles. "You're gorgeous. Have you ever thought of modeling?" He's getting closer, placing his hands around my waist. I shuffle backward as my breaths become labored; I can't deal with his proximity.

He squints at me, seeing my unease and immediately letting go of me. Before things can get weirder, my brain pushes into gear. "Modeling?" I awkwardly laugh. "I think being five-foot-one is probably a barrier to entry, no?" I'm trying to pretend that I didn't just freak out from his touch and luckily, he goes along with it.

"Touché." He snickers, dropping my mini freak-out without worry. I turn to find Vincent again. "Ah, I see." His voice is knowing. "The Bull, huh?" He raises his eyebrows at me in question, and I shrug my shoulders.

"Do you also fight?"

"Nah." He takes a sip of his drink. "My boy is tough as fuck though; he got his nickname for a reason. A lot of pent-up aggression. It works for him to get in the ring." It's clear Tom is a nice guy, but *nice* isn't on my radar right now.

I zero in on Vincent while he talks to two burly men, each standing on either side of him. They take turns talking while he stands tall, listening and nodding his head. He seems to be scanning the area, looking for something or maybe, someone. Luckily, Tom seems to take the hint as he walks away from me.

Finally, Vincent and I lock eyes again. I give him a small smile, asking— no, begging—him to come back to me. He reads me easily, walking over.

"Wanna get outta here?" His gruff voice does something to my insides. I've gone mute again and can only nod my head *yes*. I catch the gleam in his eye as he takes my hand, leading us back up the steps and into the night.

CHAPTER 6

I trail behind him with anticipation, our hands locked together. It feels so incredible to hold his hand. I wonder how it's possible that I've gone eighteen years without it.

We get outside and I wait patiently on the corner as he walks to the street to hail a taxi. One pulls up and Vincent opens the door, waiting for me to step in first. For a moment, my mind catches up with me and I hesitate.

He seems to notice my nerves. "I can take you home, or we can go somewhere to eat if you're down," he says to me gently. He's assuring me. And for some reason that I can't fully comprehend, I trust him.

I shrug my shoulders casually, believing the feeling in my gut that I'll be okay. "Sure, I can always eat." I slide into the back seat of the cab and scoot over to the far window. When the door shuts, I feel like I've got skates on my feet and I'm being propelled forward. There is no stopping what's happening to me. I'm in a taxi with a complete and utterly gorgeous stranger. I must be insane.

My buzz is simmering down, but I wish it wouldn't. I feel his gaze on me and my breathing shallows. Instead of turning toward him, I sit silently, looking out the window and watching groups of people walking around enjoying the night. My brain is still shocked that I'm sitting next to him; making eye contact would be impossible right now. Luckily, he doesn't seem to mind the quiet. From my side eye, he seems totally at ease, his long legs spread wide across the seat.

Finally, the taxi pulls up to a corner; I notice we're still in the Meatpacking District. We get out of the car in front of a restaurant, Albero Di Limoni. Next door to the restaurant, there's a club called Lemon Bar. I see a bouncer standing by the club entrance, looking imposing. There's a line of people that spans the block, trying to get in. Vincent opens the door to the restaurant for us and I move inside.

I look around, gasping at the beauty. Dark, wood paneling covers the walls; in the center of the restaurant is a row of lemon trees. Fresh lemons, ready to be picked, dangle off thin branches. The smell of the restaurant is citrus-perfect. Fresh lemon, roasted garlic, and other spices permeate the air. Vincent takes my hand, leading me to a table in the back. I can't believe I've just walked into this; it's like a dream.

"Wow, this is incredible," I say in awe as I look around the restaurant, taking in the scene. I lower myself into a plush, red-velvet chair still looking around. I notice him smiling at the fact that I'm so amazed. I want to be embarrassed at my excitement, but for some reason, he seems pleased by my reaction. The red chairs look spectacular against the backdrop of yellow lemons. I can barely believe where I am!

The waiter comes over, at first happy to see Vincent. But before he can get a word out, Vincent stares him down, his face glacial. It's almost like he's trying to communicate something to him, but I can't understand what. On one hand, I'm happy as hell not to be on the receiving end of that look. On the other hand, I'm confused as to what's going on here. The waiter clears his throat, asking what we'd like to eat—a perfect professional.

"We're going to have a bottle of Pellegrino and she'll have a glass of Sancerre. She'll also have a filet steak, medium rare. Also, the Cornish hen. Side of roasted potatoes and green beans. Let's do mashed potatoes too. You know what, also bring her a salad to start. I'll have the wild salmon, simply grilled with no butter, no oil, no salt, and steamed broccoli on the side, also no butter, no oil, no salt." The waiter rushes off.

"Wow, that's a lot of food." I lift my eyebrows at him, feeling over-whelmed. I'm not used to eating out and if I do, it's usually at McDonald's. I clasp my hands together nervously under the table; I can't imagine how much this dinner must cost.

"Yeah, I guess so. I wasn't sure what you'd like. Anyway, the food's great. You'll enjoy it. I know the owner… personally." He leans forward with his elbows on the table.

I'm not sure what to say, so I go with something simple. "No butter, huh?" I smile. I'm doing my best to look into his eyes without melting into a puddle.

He laughs at my question, not bothering to answer. He looks pretty rough and I see some scratches on his jaw.

I turn toward the waiter as he places a salad and cold glass of wine in front of me. Vincent looks down at my food expectantly, waiting for me to start eating. I take the fork and dig in. The lettuce is so crispy and perfectly chilled, and the dressing tastes like mustard and vinegar. It's simply incredible. When I sip the wine, I hum. My taste buds are in a very happy place right now. "So, I take it you workout a lot?" I ask, trying to go for another easy conversation topic.

He seems bored with my question, licking his lips and glancing around the room. "Yeah, I've been doing MMA for a while now." I stay quiet, waiting for him to continue. But a few minutes of silence, I realize that he isn't going to answer me.

"Do you plan on going pro or something?"

"Nah. I just do it for fun, actually. It started with me just messing around and sort of grew from there."

Our conversation seems to halt after that. Luckily, the wine seemed to numb any filters I usually have. Before I can think twice, I open my big mouth and ask, "So, what do you think about all the problems going on in the Middle East?" His eyes widen, and he starts to laugh. I'm relieved my attempt to shake him out of his seriousness worked. He probably thinks I'm a dork now but well, whatever.

Without hesitating, he leans closer to me. "I gotta say that Netanyahu doesn't mess around. He's all about keeping Israel safe and I gotta respect that. Yeah, he pushes boundaries. And the UN hates Israel's guts, that's for sure…" His voice trails off, but my heart starts to pound.

I lean forward, putting my elbows on the table. "Have you read his autobiography? Netanyahu's, I mean. I went through a phase where I was trying to understand the Middle Eastern conflict better. It was actually really good."

"Believe it or not, it's sitting on my desk. I usually buy ten or fifteen books at a time and tell myself that I've got to finish them within the year. I just finished *The Autobiography of Malcolm X*."

I swallow hard. "I read that," I tell him quietly. My heart is filling up; that's one of the most influential books of my life. Thoughts of my childhood reading partner, Javi, enter my mind, and all of a sudden, I feel a combination of hot and terrified.

His throat moves as he drinks from his cup of water. "Yeah? What did you think?" He places the glass down, entirely focused and waiting for my reply. I'm not used to this type of conversation, and it's both nerve-wracking and exciting. He's looking at me as if he's actually interested to hear what I have to say. Even though I'm scared to sound stupid, a large part of me yearns to rise up. I push away any anxiety and reply.

"Most people stick to what they know because they don't know that any better option exists. They have no one in their lives who shows them a path that's different from the one they see everyone around them taking. Or, they make certain choices in their youth that result in shutting down any possibilities for the future. By the time they get older and understand the mistake, it's too late to back out. They're incarcerated or dead. Or maybe they're involved in some gang that won't let them out."

He chimes in. "But sometimes, things happen to us that propels us toward a different destiny. And I think that when Malcolm X goes to jail and makes a conscious choice to refrain from eating pork, that one small act was the catalyst in changing the entire course of his life. So, change is possible, right? If, of course, you can survive long enough to get to that point." He's staring at me seriously, and this time the feeling goes way beyond the physical. I'm gazing into his dark eyes, and somehow, his presence makes me want to rise up in all senses of the word.

I swallow again. His expression turns thoughtful, as if he's really waiting to hear my reply. I want to show him what I think; I feel as if I don't have to hide with this man. I push my worry in the back of my mind again, and allow myself to speak freely. The alcohol is definitely helping the situation, shutting up my nerves and loosening my tongue.

"I hear your idealism. And I know it seems possible to believe we can all change, especially when reading about a man like Malcolm X. But for most people, experiencing a world outside of their poverty is near to impossible. I mean, it's easy for a rich guy to believe that a kid from the ghetto can turn his life around if he just stopped with the violence, or picked up a book, or got into religion. But, you can't protect yourself from violence with a book.

The streets are dangerous, Vincent. And most people do the best they can to protect themselves. And when protection is on your mind, and feeding your family—or when other basic necessities are at risk—there is no time for introspection or higher knowledge. That makes changing really, really difficult, although not impossible."

"Well, jail is certainly a place where you have nothing else to do but think and reach higher knowledge, huh?" He exaggerates his shrug, and I start to laugh.

A flicker of amusement passes through his face at my reaction, but his stare somehow intensifies. I feel my face growing red.

He continues. "Well, let's get real for a second. If you're willing to die to get out of your circumstances, that may be the answer. I mean, you can easily say, fuck it. Forget protection and basic necessities. Forget being smart on the street. My goal is getting out, even if I may die trying."

I'm in a state of utter shock right now and I'm sure my face shows it, because he's smiling like he just won a game. I'm not sure if he realizes that he just pegged me, but he did. He hit my nail on the head.

I take another huge swallow of my wine. "Well, what do you make of the fact that once Malcolm X finally found peace, he was assassinated?"

He leans forward, even closer. "I think that America likes to claim that in this country, there's mobility within the classes. But in reality, even if you transcend your upbringing, there's someone who will push you back down again. Maybe in reality, change is actually impossible."

"No!" I exclaim, dropping my fork onto my plate. His eyes widen in surprise at my outburst, but I can't believe that what he's saying is true. "Change has to be possible…" I turn my head down, trying to process my thoughts.

"Eve," he starts. "It's not just people in poverty who suffer from this… I mean, shit, there's always someone controlling all of us. None of us are really free, are we? In every single realm from impoverished up to Arab Sheiks, we're all victims of how we were raised. Did you read *The Short and Tragic Life of Robert Peace?*" I nod my head.

"He may not have been assassinated, but he was brought back down and into the rabbit hole of his upbringing, regardless of the Ivy League college he attended and all the schooling in the world combined with incredible natural brilliance. Because change is—"

"No," I stop him. "Change is not impossible. It has to be possible! And yeah, I see what you're saying. But Rob didn't have to sell drugs. He chose it in the end, and that was his downfall. His bad choice. His refusal to let go of where he came from."

"So, you're saying that if you want to change, you need to cut ties with your past?"

"Yes." I nod vigorously. "I do. I think that sometimes you need to burn bridges. I think that in order to transcend a life of poverty, you've got to do just that—leave the hood behind."

"But what if your past isn't necessarily bad blood? Like, maybe you're poor and live in the ghetto, but you've got a huge amazing family. You still want out, though. Do you have to leave all those people behind? It's not always one-dimensional."

I immediately think of some friends from the Blue Houses, with huge but loving families. "Well, yeah. I think you can bring them into your new life, but I don't think going back to your old life is smart. You'd be surprised at how impoverished cultures aren't interested or supportive of people breaking out of the mold; it's almost as if they feel like if you leave the community, you're denying their value. Like, if you leave, it's because you don't think they're good enough or worth staying for. It's offensive to them. Maybe your own family is supportive and proud. But the community as a whole, not so much."

He stops and we get quiet, looking at each other. My chest constricts from the intensity of our conversation, and he looks at me with all the interest a set of eyes can convey. Deep down, I feel angry and upset. He doesn't know that I'm that person. I'm that girl with nothing and a shitty upbringing. I'm the one who is willing to die trying.

"Eve, look at me." I bring my gaze back up to his. "I wasn't trying to say that it's impossible to change. I mean…" he swallows. "I'm not poor by any stretch," he admits. "But, I've been raised in a certain way. I've also made choices that were in line with expectations placed on me. I've also picked a path that maybe, under other circumstances, I wouldn't have chosen. But now I'm here. In that life. And there's no way out."

I'm surprised by his admission, but assume that he's talking about being forced into grad school or something. A man like him doesn't have real problems. I mean, look at the place he brought me! Everything about him screams confidence and money.

"But Vincent, you don't have to live that way if you don't want to. You can wake up one morning and leave. You aren't behind bars or dead. You aren't in some gang where the only way out is in a body bag."

He pulls his head back, looking as if I've slapped him. Maybe I said something that touched too close to home. I want to say more, but before I can continue, dish after dish comes out of the kitchen and onto our beautiful table. I can't help myself as I dig into the delicious food. He watches me quietly as I eat my dinner. We're silent, and I'm glad for that. The silence with him is comfortable and somehow, full of warmth. We went from challenging each other to enjoying each other.

I've never eaten a filet steak in my life, and the meat melts in my mouth like butter. I moan from the taste, and he gives me a heated look.

"What?" I ask him, smiling with my mouth full, taking another sip of the cold wine. I look at my glass and realize that somehow, despite how much I've drunk, my glass is still full.

He leans closer to me. "Watching you eat is... let's just say that I don't usually see girls enjoying food like you do. I like it." His voice is a whisper, and I feel it straight down into my core.

I put my fork down and lick my lips, feeling the urge to engage him once again. "Yeah, you're probably used to girls picking at their salads, huh? No butter, no salt, no pepper, no taste?" I reply, starting to laugh. I'd be lying if I said I wasn't enjoying the hell out of the moment. Apparently with Vincent, I can go from serious conversation to banter in a matter of minutes.

"Oh baby, you have no idea. Between my usual clean food diet and these super skinny girls I'm normally with, we're like a restaurant's worst night-mare." Realizing he's making fun of himself, I can't help the giggle that erupts from my mouth. He chuckles with wonder when he sees my face.

"So, are you saying I'm not super skinny?" I raise my eyebrows, daring him to call me fat.

He drinks me in with his eyes, staring at me from my face down to my chest and back up again. "You're perfect; that's what you are." I open my mouth and then snap it shut.

"You know, when I saw you enter the ring, I was afraid for a few seconds. That meathead was practically foaming at the mouth." I cut up another piece of steak.

He snorts. "Yeah and that name Jack *the Ripper*?" Putting his fork into his food, he takes another large bite.

"Yeah," I nod enthusiastically. "That name is too ridiculous to take seriously." I roll my eyes, putting the meat in my mouth and moaning again. He looks at me incredulously as if I'm groaning for his sake. I ignore him and keep eating; nothing is going to stop me from enjoying this incredible meal. Just a few hours ago, I was sitting in my shitty apartment, eating Dominos with my sister. And now here I am, eating a however-many-course meal with the most gorgeous and intelligent man I've ever laid eyes on!

My mouth is full, but I continue, "I mean, I can think of a hundred better names than that stupid one." I swallow, clearing my throat. "If I were a fighter, I'd call myself *the Raven*." I can't help the smile that forms on my face.

He chuckles. "Is that your alter ego?" He's joking around with me and I... well, I freakin' love it!

"Oh yeah, that's me...poverty-stricken-book-nerd by day, pecking on people's windows by night and scaring the crap out of them," I deadpan.

He laughs out loud and the sound fills up a spot inside my chest. The table next to us turns around, but I barely register them. All I can see is the man sitting in front of me.

"Or you can go really wild and call yourself Poe's Raven." He's waiting for me to catch his drift and I'm squealing for joy inside. I want to scream, *I'm nerdy too! I know the poem!*

I can't help myself but recite it. I'm just really dorky like that and apparently, drunk enough to show it. "Once upon a midnight dreary, while I pondered, weak and weary..."

He stops me, a look of shock passing over his chiseled features. "Over many a quaint and curious volume of forgotten lore—"

My eyes widen and he guffaws. We're quoting poetry right now and my heart is so full I want to jump up and down and scream. Who the hell is this man? No, really. Who? An MMA fighter from an underground fighting ring?

A poet? A few seconds pass. Or maybe it's minutes. But we're quiet, staring into each other's eyes. We're not even waiting for someone to talk. We're just staring. Glowing. Something is passing between us that I can't rationally explain.

Before I can stop myself, my subconscious blurts out, "Do you see me?" I immediately drop my head, shocked I just said that out loud. I'm not even sure what I meant! I turn red again, embarrassment blazing. I risk a glance at Vincent only to see him grinning, apparently pleased by my word vomit.

He moves forward in his chair, leaning closer to me. "Yes, Eve. I see you. And for the record, I like what I see. A lot." His eyes actually twinkle with his words. It dawns on me that this may be the first time I've ever been truly looked at. I never knew how much I ached for this feeling, until now.

"How did you get the name *the Bull*, anyway?" I'm smiling so wide that my cheeks are starting to ache.

"Well, you want the true story or the story I tell people?"

"Hmm." I press my lips together and stare at the ceiling, as if deep in thought. "Give me the truth." I stare into his eyes. "Always the truth." I drop my elbows on the table, not wanting to miss a word.

"How about I tell you both. And you tell me which one is real and which is the lie?" I nod my head, excited to play along.

"All right," he clears his throat. "Once upon a time, Zeus sees Europa. The second his eyes are on her, he knows he wants her. But he also knows she would never come to him out of her own free will. So, one day he disguises himself as a beautiful white bull. After a few minutes of petting the bull, she decides to sit on him, expecting him to be as gentle as he is beautiful. But as she sits on the bull's back, he runs away, stealing her and bringing her to Crete." He takes another bite of his food. "So basically, Zeus saw what he wanted, and he found a way to take her." After swallowing, he lifts a glass of water to his lips.

"Um, doesn't the story go that he steals and *rapes* her?" I ask, my eyebrows furrowing together.

He's silent until bursting into laughter, clapping his hands like my response was the funniest thing he's ever heard. "You little genius, huh? When can I watch you on Jeopardy?" His smile is blinding me. He's playing with me, but he isn't being condescending. I've never had more fun in my entire life.

I roll my eyes. "I do know a ton of useless shit. I gotta call them and get on that show." He's shaking his head incredulously, and I can't stop myself from smiling. Gah!

"Well," he clears his throat. "Some people say it ended in a rape. But I don't believe that. He just took what he wanted and didn't let anyone stop him."

I smirk. "All right. So, you're the bull who looks all perfect, but really, you're a selfish god? Totally possible for you to believe that about yourself, cocky bastard you obviously are. And what's the second story?" He's staring at me as if I'm something special. My heart warms. No, it's not warming. It's actually on fire right now. I feel like a side of myself, which I've never dared to show, has been brought out of me. I wish it would never end.

"Well, believe it or not, I wasn't always this big." I make a face, ready to call bullshit. I can't imagine him ever being small.

"Just listen. I was in second grade, and I was getting picked on at recess. This kid, Jack Ford, kept pushing me around with some of his friends. At first, I tried to ignore them. But somehow a shadow came over me and I went berserk. I fought the kids and took them all down, breaking one of their noses in the process. Not that I knew any fighting skills, but I was an angry little shit. Apparently, everyone who watched me said I looked like an angry bull. The name stuck."

I sit back in my chair, looking at him intently. "I don't know which story is real. Both seem kind of plausible." I'm about to take another bite of the steak, but stop before it reaches my lips. "Stop staring at me, Vincent! I'm sorry for the moaning and groaning, but it's just too good! You have to try some." I hand him my fork. He takes it from my hand, placing the meat in his mouth. He lets out a grumble as he chews, the sound coming from deep in his throat. All kinds of signals are sent straight from my ears down through my body.

His eyes move above my head and he squints, looking surprised at whatever he sees. I turn around, wondering what it is he saw. A group of men have come into the restaurant, all in dark suits. Most of the people eating turn around to stare at them; their presence is noticeable.

"We should go," he tells me abruptly, standing and waiting for me to grab my purse off the back of my chair. Without even asking for the check, he lifts my hand into his and we jet through the restaurant, still completely filled with people. I'm confused, but too nervous and uncomfortable to ask what the hell is going on. I guess he did say he knows the owner—I assume he'll pay later.

While Vincent hails another taxi, I look behind me to see the line for Lemon Bar has doubled. I know how weird it is that I'm born and raised in New York City, but never went to a nightclub. Maybe I'll go soon with Janelle. I turn my head, ready to abandon thoughts of dancing when Vincent moves next to me.

He looks back and forth between the door of the club and the restaurant. "You want to go inside?" His smile is infectious and before I know it, I'm nodding my head *yes*. It seems whatever had him running isn't following us out. Looking at some people handing their ID's to the bouncer, it dawns on me this club is probably for twenty-one and over.

"I don't have an ID. You need that to get in, right?" I'm not even sure how old Vincent is, but he definitely looks older than I am.

"You don't need an ID when you're with me." His smile is so warm. "Come on, let's go

have some fun."

Before we move, I ask, "How old are you, Vincent?"

He grins, as if my question amuses him. "I'm a junior in college." My heart skips at the word *college*.

The bouncer notices Vincent and immediately stops, opening up the velvet rope for us to pass through. I hear some people grumble with annoyance, but Vincent struts forward like he owns the place. We get inside the club and walk straight to the bar. The room is completely packed, but he easily slides himself between two people to get a spot.

He turns to me. "You want water or another drink?" I'm already feeling more than buzzed from the wine at dinner. "Um, just water, please." He nods his head, seemingly happy at my response. The bartender trips over herself to get to Vincent, and I grimace.

After I take a few sips, he drops my glass on the bar and takes my hand, bringing me to the center of the dance floor. I start to move, but I'm relieved to see that he's kept a slight distance. The music is amazing and I can feel the bass in the center of my chest. Throngs of people surround us, and it's easy to just get lost in the mix. Before I know it, I'm completely letting go and dancing with my whole body. His hands move around my waist, but he still isn't bringing me flush against his chest like I wish he would. A few times I try to move closer to him, but he's in total control. I want to be upset that he doesn't want to feel me against him, but I'm too happy to let myself pout.

I touch my shoulder, feeling the dampness on my skin. Looking up into his face, I notice he's hot as well. I've never had fun like this in my life!

He puts his hand in his back pocket, pulling out his phone and looking at it closely. "I've got to make a quick call. Wait for me, okay?" he's yelling over the music, and I hear him clearly. He leads me back to the center of the bar. "Don't move!" He winks, giving my hand a squeeze before walking off. At first, I see his dark head over everyone else, but then he's gone. I'm standing and minding my own business when a man I don't know slides up next to me.

"Hey, sweetheart. Can I buy you a drink?" I barely notice anything other than he's tall with blond hair when I reply.

"No, thank you." I keep my back straight and turn my head away from him, not wanting to give him any ideas.

"Come on, baby. Let me buy you something." He tries to get closer and I immediately feel my body tighten with anxiety. I want to move backward, but the bar is so full of people, the only way I can escape him is to leave the bar entirely—and if I exit this area, what if I don't find Vincent again? It occurs to me Vincent may have left me here. What if his plan was to ditch me and he doesn't come back at all? I mean, sure we've been having a great time. But he doesn't owe me anything. Janelle has told me about countless guys who she thought were crazy about her, but ultimately left her high and dry. I'm sweating again, except this time, it isn't from chemistry or the heat of the room. I check my watch, realizing it's getting close to two and I'm all alone. I didn't even consider how I'm going to get back into my apartment. I need to call Janelle, but my hands are shaking too badly.

After taking a good look at me, the man's flirtation turns into concern. "Hey, sweetie, are you all right? I wasn't tryin' to upset you. Look, let me get you some water. Calm down, okay? I had a girlfriend once who had bad anxiety." He turns to flag down the bartender. He orders me a cup of tap and I swallow it down.

"Feeling better?" I blink a few times, wanting to reply. I'm afraid if I open my mouth, I'll burst into tears. I never should have come here with a complete stranger. I never should have drunk any alcohol. I'm clearly inept at judging situations. I'm obviously incompetent, just like my mom always says.

"Take a few deep breaths," he instructs calmly. I'm holding onto the edge of the bar, my knuckles turning white. "Do you have a friend here? Maybe we should get some fresh air." I nod, but still can't manage speech. I turn around to leave when Vincent steps in front of me.

I must look like I'm having some sort of panic attack, because his wide smile turns down the second he sees the state I'm in. "You okay, baby? What the fuck happened here?" My bar neighbor turns to him to say something but freezes when he sees the look on Vincent's face.

"Did this guy mess with you?" Vincent's aggression should be making everything worse. Instead, I feel the anxiety drain from the soles of my feet. I grab his shirt, turning him toward me before he gets in this guy's face.

"No, Vincent, I—" My body trembles as relief courses through me. Vincent is back. Half of me wants to jump into his arms and thank him for not disappearing. But the other half wants to smack him across the face for walking away in the first place.

He leans into me, putting a hand on my arm to calm me down. "Let me take you home, okay? I shouldn't have left you alone—"

"I'm not a regular in places like these…" I'm moving my head from side to side, trying not to sound desperate. But the truth is I'm scared as hell. This is too much too soon.

He nods his head and grips my hand tightly, letting me know without words that it's okay. We walk out of the club together and back onto the street corner. Even though it's late, the block is full of people. He continues to hold my hand as he lifts his free arm to hail a taxi; one immediately pulls up to the corner.

Vincent opens the door for me and I climb inside first, moving to the far window. He follows me into the back seat, sitting flush against me. I feel his thigh pressing against mine; I'm not sure what I should do. Should I move my leg? Stay where I am? Does he notice what he's doing, or am I just over-thinking it? Maybe this is how he normally sits, with his huge, muscular thigh touching the person next to him? I look up at him and he turns his face to mine. It dawns on me this man is used to getting everything he wants, when-ever he wants it. I'm nervous, but holy shit do I want to please him. The real-ization is instantly sobering. I can't look away from his dark, gorgeous eyes.

The driver bangs his steering wheel, his voice instantly breaking our mo-ment. "Where you headed?" he asks in a heavy Middle Eastern accent.

We both turn toward him. "I'm on Avenue D and Fifth," I reply. My voice doesn't falter, but I'm nervous, hoping Vincent doesn't recognize the address.

Sure enough, though, his eyes widen in disbelief. "You're in the Blue Houses?" The tone of his voice is unmistakable; he's surprised and seems to pity me.

"Yeah." I look back at him, shrugging my shoulders. I want to tell him sure, *it's a pretty horrible place to live, but it's home for now.* As I turn away from him to stare out the window, he takes my hand and gently rubs his cal-lused thumb back and forth over my knuckles. It's both soothing and arousing at once. I swallow hard, trying to steady my heart rate. I cross my legs and let out a sigh, keeping my eyes focused on the city streets.

A few minutes later, the cab stops short in front of my building. I let my-self out of the back seat and look up, wondering what it looks like to an out-sider. Three tall gray buildings are clustered together and fenced-in balconies

77

frame the facade. The result is a prison-like structure. Pockets of people stand around smoking. On a night like this one, with clear skies, people don't like to sit in their small apartments. I see a couple of guys on the stoop, observing everyone coming and going from the entrance. Luckily, they aren't wearing any colors; I know they may be thugs, but they aren't gang affiliated.

Vincent swipes his credit card to pay the taxi driver and steps out, insisting on walking me to the building's front door. I want to protest to prove that I'm independent, but my innate sense of self-preservation tells me not to let him go. Even though there are people around, it's late and dark—and being alone, even if I'm armed, isn't the brightest idea. He slightly raises his chin, looking straight-up lethal. The intelligent man from the restaurant is gone, and in his place is the Bull from the ring.

Taking my hand, Vincent walks us inside the building with purpose, as if he's the one who lives here. He makes it clear that he's taking me all the way up to my apartment's front door; he's a man on a mission, and I'm not planning on stopping him.

He opens the door for me and we walk into the dingy gray lobby. The elevator has a sign on the door that says: OUT OF ORDER. I shut my eyes, cursing my luck. Looks like we'll have to walk up the steps—just another sign pointing to my background, unworthy of a man like him. I lead him to the stairwell. Like a bad horror film, the lights flicker when the door slams shut. The light settles on a dim glow. He stops at the base of the steps, squeezing my hand and cursing. "This is dangerous. Tell me the lights normally work."

"Uh, maybe I should tell you two stories. One real and one made up. You tell me which is which." I internally slap myself five for giving back what he gave me just a few hours earlier.

He chuckles. "Okay." We begin the trek up the steps. Luckily, he can't see my face right now, because my body short-circuits every time his chest or hand brushes my back. It feels like I'm being stalked up the stairs; he's just so close, but at the same time, not nearly close enough.

I try to sound upbeat. "There's a fantastic super who fixes everything anytime tenants call. I'm sure all the bulbs will be replaced by morning." He lets out a noncommittal grunt.

"Ready for the second story?" Our pace seems to be slowing down as his hand lightly grazes my lower back. He continues to touch me, and I get the feeling it isn't by accident.

"Go on." His voice is rough, and I blink a few times to steady myself.

"I'm lucky the light is even flickering. Sometimes it gets so dark, I may as well be walking through a black tube."

I stop when we get to the fourth floor, turning around at the top step to tell him this is it. Before I can continue our little game to ask him which story is the truth, he puts his hands on my waist, waiting for me to look up at him.

I may be standing on a step above him, but he still towers over me. I watch as he licks his full lips, and my core begins to pulse from the visual. I'm not sure what the hell is happening to me, but my mind can't focus on anything other than Vincent. The darkness is impairing my vision, resulting in a heightening of all of my other senses. I put my hands around his neck and feel the warm sinewy muscle under my fingers. With both his hands, he pushes my hair behind my ears and angles my head up to face him. He's asking me with his touch if I want this. I let out a loud sigh and lean toward him as every cell in my body screams *YES*.

When he presses his lips to mine, I freeze. But he doesn't let it deter him. Instead, he continues kissing me with a surprising gentleness, moving his mouth against mine and finally sliding his tongue alongside the seam of my mouth, begging entrance.

I open my mouth, letting him inside. His taste combined with the softness of his tongue has my legs weakening. He wraps a strong arm around my waist and holds me up, steadying me. Within seconds, his soft kisses become demanding. I'm trying to keep up with his pace, but it feels so good, all I can do is take it. He lifts me up and I instinctually wrap my legs around his waist. As if I weigh nothing at all, he walks us up to the landing and pushes me against the concrete wall. My phone drops to the ground, but I barely hear it or notice. He starts to rub against me rhythmically, pressing his hardness against my jeans in slow and deep strokes. I let out a moan as he hits a spot that's starting an electrical current in my veins. Sweat beads on the back of my neck and between my breasts. My body is on overload; heat traveling from where he's pushing against me out into all of my limbs. I'm shaking as my hands clutch his strong shoulders. He moves his lips from my mouth to my neck and I lean my head back against the wall, offering myself to him. God, it feels so good. Too good. Moments later, his lips suck a trail up to my ear. I'm burning up.

His lips move to my ear. "Fucking gorgeous, baby. Watching you dance, I had to talk myself down from taking you right there in the middle of the club." Replying is not possible; the only sounds coming from my lips are moans.

My body is climbing higher and higher toward something. I feel him unbuttoning my jeans and I'm letting him. I'd do anything to soothe this ache. And right when I think I'm about to incinerate, his hand reaches down and presses into a spot that literally short circuits my brain. My head slams against the wall behind me and I'm completely lost, a scream tearing from my throat. I have zero control as my body melts on and on. He holds onto me, wrapping his body around me tightly as I come down from the high.

"What the hell was that?" I pant. I can barely see him as the lights flicker on and off, but the questioning look he gives me is clear.

"Was that your first orgasm, Eve?" All I can do is nod my head. He sighs, dropping his head into the crook of my neck. "God, baby. I can't lie to you. I like that. I like that a lot. You're so innocent and stunning. Fuck." My eyes close again when I feel his lips back on mine, his tongue slowly dragging in and out of my mouth.

I let out a hum and give myself over to him; I'm so pliable right now; he could do anything he wanted, and I would say *yes*. When he pulls back, I open my eyes and touch my hands to my face, noticing how hot it is to the touch. He slowly lowers my feet to the ground and all I want to do is beg him to keep me up here, close to his body. I button my jeans as he bends down, picking up my phone and handing it to me.

We walk together to my apartment door. I turn toward him and look up into his intense eyes, wanting to thank him. But when I hear a couple fighting, I'm immediately brought back to my reality. I drop my head, irrationally wishing he either didn't hear or didn't notice. I'm one-hundred percent sure this isn't the type of place Vincent is used to.

Noticing my discomfort, he slowly lifts my head back up. "Hey, Eve. Look at me." My eyes meet his again. "Give me your phone and let me give you my number." He waits patiently for me to pull out my phone.

I reach into my purse and hand it to him, breathing deeply. All of a sudden, things have gotten quiet between us.

He opens my contacts and types his information. I'm pressing my lips together, waiting for him to ask me for my number in return. But when he hands me back my phone, I can't manage any words. Leaning against the doorway, he looks down at me and pushes some errant hair out of my face. "You're different from other girls I know." Licking his lips, he bends down, pressing a chaste kiss on my forehead. "I'll see you around, okay? Promise you'll call me if you ever need anything." He turns around to leave, and I'm stuck speechless and quaking.

I float into my apartment, my brain short-circuited and high, but sublimely happy. I go into the bathroom to wash up, wishing I could savor this feeling for eternity. Before removing my makeup, I look in the mirror. Staring at myself, I try to see what he could possibly see in me.

My eyes shine brown and my hair looks glossy and full. My lips are puffy and pink from all the kissing. I touch my lips and sigh. When I'm all clean, I get into bed, replaying my night over and over. If I sleep, will it all just disappear? I try to keep myself awake to prolong the feeling and the memories, but with enough time, my body gives into exhaustion and I fall asleep.

CHAPTER 7

Saturday morning comes too quickly. By the time I wake up, Janelle has already left for work. I wash up as fast as I can, not wanting to be late for my meeting with Ms. Levine at her apartment. I take the Six Train Uptown to Eighty-Sixth Street and walk out of the station, immediately coming face to face with Ms. Levine's tall glass building—a gorgeous brand-new condominium called the Lucinda.

I have a definite bounce in my step today. I'm not sure I'll ever see Vincent again, but just the potential is enough to lift up my spirits. I can barely believe a man like him exists in this world. I also can't believe all of the incredible things he made me feel. *He's here in this city,* my heart whispers. Maybe my luck is finally changing? I feel the hope move around in my chest.I stop at the desk in Ms. Levine's fancy lobby, letting the concierge know who I'm here to see. I turn my head to the front door as a bellboy pushes a large cart filled with suitcases. "The car should be out front," the woman tells him with a stony face.

Ms. Levine used to make some serious bank as a high-powered attorney in the city but left her white-glove life to help the city's neediest kids change their lives. Unfortunately for her, aid is almost impossible to give in a school system that's utterly broken and with kids who refuse to change. But I guess, there's me. And there's no denying the fact that she's changing the hell out of my life.

I remember when she walked into my ninth-grade English class. We all knew she was a brand-new teacher, and most of the students were ready to give her their version of a warm welcome. She walked into the classroom in a designer-looking suit and high heels that screamed, "I'm ready to take on the world!" Before she could put her briefcase on the chair by her desk, someone launched a calculator at her head. Laughter ensued, but it was just the beginning.

By her fourth day, kids were throwing textbooks from the fifth-story classroom window. It's safe to say her idealism took a hit pretty early on in her teaching career.

Even though the classroom drama persisted, she still assigned *The Great Gatsby* as the first required reading, followed by an essay on the book's portrayal of the upper versus lower classes of society. Because I happen to love that book and read it with my old friend Javi in eighth grade, I wrote the paper. I handed it to her quietly after class, writing: PLEASE DON'T TELL ANYONE I WROTE THIS at the top. The last thing I needed was to draw negative attention to myself.

Javi Dante was a friend of mine. He was *smart*. We'd pass books between ourselves—hiding the books as if we had cash inside our backpacks—reading for pleasure and for the possibility of a better life one day. Our hunger to get the hell out of the Blue Houses was insatiable. We would stick Post-Its inside the pages of borrowed classics, scribbling notes to each other. We read everything we could get our hands on. Malcolm X. Paulo Coehelo. Zora Neal Hurston.

The morning of his death, I passed him *The Invisible Man*—a book that shook me to the core but was ultimately left undiscussed. The cops found the book in his bag, wondering who wrote on all the green Post-Its. No one ever found out it was me. Janelle knew everything, though. She told me to shut up and stay low for a while. People can smell the stench of potential, and somehow, it never ended well for most of them.

The community went crazy for a few weeks, wondering who killed this innocent boy.

"Another youth wasted!"

"He had the highest grades for math. He could have been a doctor!"

"His mom applied him to one of the best prep schools in the country; they already accepted him for high school!"

"He could have been something. Done something for this comm-u-nity!"

"We need better schools. Someone, tell the mayor!"

It all fell on deaf ears. Debts are owed, and sometimes lives are used as payment. Here, our bodies are nothing but currency. I later found out his brother cheated the Snakes out of some drug money. To show their power, his brother had to pay in blood. Javi was the blood.

A few days after I handed in the paper, Ms. Levine pulled me aside and insisted my intelligence was being neglected; she wasn't going to stand for it any longer. According to her, I was never able to translate my intellect into academic potential. She intended on being the one to change that.

Since then, Ms. Levine has been on a mission to get me out of the ghetto and into an Ivy League college—insisting with her help, I could change the path of my life.

In the past three years, our relationship has grown from teacher and student to mentor and mentee. She's had my sister Janelle and me over to her beautiful apartment for countless dinners and gives us all sorts of advice, which goes way beyond the academic. When Janelle had a pregnancy scare last year, Ms. Levine's apartment was where she took her First Response test, which was thankfully negative. And when my mom came home on a drug-induced rampage and cut up all of my clothes with meat scissors, Ms. Levine is the one who brought me to Target on 117th street and replaced all of my old thrift-shop clothes.

Finally, the concierge nods at me, letting me know without a word that I can head up. Stepping into the wood-paneled elevator, it brings me directly to the fifteenth floor.

I walk down the carpeted hallway when her door swings open. "Hi, Eve! Application time!" she says in a sing-song voice. She hugs me tightly, genuinely happy to have me here. Ms. Levine is tall and thin with long caramel-colored hair. Normally, she wears it in a tight bun; right now, it's down around her face, making her look much younger.

"Eve, I already printed out ten copies of your transcript. I made copies of your best essay to attach to each application as a writing sample, and I wrote you a recommendation letter, which I really think is going to be the kicker!" Her voice rings with excitement as she brings me over to her dining table, grabbing stacks of papers off the console.

The apartment is modern and sleek with floor-to-ceiling glass windows on the entire west side. I look out at the city streets, wondering for the millionth time what it would be like to have an apartment this perfect and safe. One day, maybe.

I turn around, walking toward the wall where a large rectangular Peter Lik photograph hangs: a huge tree stands tall, the sun shining like a star through lustrous orange and red leaves. Living in a concrete jungle, I love seeing nature, even if it's only in a photograph. I'm shaken out of my fog when she hands me a plate of hot eggs, bacon, and toast.

"Take this and eat, you'll need your energy up for us to work." She stares at me expectantly with a huge smile on her face, but I'm confused by her demeanor. She's always kind, yet all of this feels a bit contrived. I take a seat at the dining table while she sits across from me. She's staring straight at me, seemingly waiting for something. The moment I see the pity and sadness pass through her eyes, I realize she knows about what happened with Carlos. I try to find the words to ask her about her day. I want to change the subject, but tears run without my consent down my face. She moves to the chair next to me as I crumble into her arms, looking for solace. She hugs me close to her, supporting me.

"Janelle explained everything already; she called me last week. Just... calm down, we're going to get you out of this."

I look up, worry sinking into my gut. "Are you going to tell someone about what happened to me? If you do, there's no way I'll live to see the day..." My breaths become shallow as my panic rises.

She drops a warm hand on my shoulder. "Eve, please calm down. I won't tell, okay? I know how things work here. I could get into serious trouble for not telling the authorities, but I'll take that risk for you."

My crying intensifies as relief sets into my chest. "This is the plan," she starts. "We're going to get you into college and out of here. A summer program, first. We're applying to these ten schools." She gestures to the paperwork already organized and laid out in the center of the table. "I'm using school funds for your application fees, so we can apply anywhere you want. And I've already cleared it with the principal; so don't worry about the money. You've got to hang on for six more months, and then you're free." I nod my head, swallowing. "You think you can lay low and out of harm's way until we get you out?"

My mind starts to race. "But what if I don't get the scholarship and grant money? I can't have Janelle support me anymore—"

"You took your SATs, and you did unbelievably well. I know you'll qualify for a full scholarship. And we both know it's highly likely Columbia will accept you. You know I've got pull at that school. There are so many grants and scholarships available you qualify for. I mean, if not for you, who the heck would that money be for?"

I chuckle, shrugging my shoulders. She has a point. "The thing is, I can't just keep letting Janelle handle paying for me. I'm letting you know now if I can't find a school that'll hook me up financially, I'm not going."

She puts her hands on mine. "You'll get it, Eve. You'll get it and you'll get the hell out of here." She takes a deep breath. "Have you spoken to your mom about college?" I raise my eyebrows at her in surprise and annoyance.

"Okay." She lifts her hand up as if to say she won't harp on the subject. "Let's just forget your mom for now. You know what? Forget everything. Let's just start by applying. When you get in, we'll figure out how to make it happen. You're a brilliant girl, and it's time to put that brain of yours in a place that's right for you."

I look down at my feet; my boots are Janelle's hand-me-downs. They've got a few holes in the heel, but since I lost my sneakers, I've had to make do. I know Janelle would easily give me the cash to buy a new pair, but the guilt I feel from taking money from her at this point is enormous. My job at Angelo's is okay, but two days a week isn't enough to give me much spending cash. I need to get those grants and the full scholarship. And maybe Ms. Levine is right; if not for me, who would it be for?

We spend the rest of the afternoon filling out applications, making sure to include everything the schools requested. Grant applications take even more time, as do the applications for scholarships. Ms. Levine wasn't kidding; there are so many places willing to give money to a kid like me. I just need to stay organized. Ms. Levine has a large spreadsheet detailing what we need and what we've taken care of, so we don't lose track. Without her, I'd be completely lost.

"Ms. Levine, do you think I'll fit into these places? I mean, no one I know has ever gone to college, and…" I feel insecurity pounding in my chest. "I mean, I know I'm different from the people I grew up around. But, that doesn't mean I'm gonna fit in with people like *them*," I say, pointing to the picture on the brochure folder for Columbia University. College kids in Polo shirts are throwing Frisbees to one another on a beautiful green campus lawn. "I've never touched a Frisbee in my life…. And like, what about Janelle? I'm nervous to leave her—"

She cuts me off. "Listen, Eve. Don't feel guilty about leaving. Imagine the life you will bring to yourself and Janelle once you graduate college. Doors will open. Law school, like you've always dreamed! I've lived that life, and I know you can make it there. And, Janelle wants this so badly for you…"

I take a breath and gather my thoughts. Images of my mom barge into my head, unwelcome. "You know my mom would go insane if she thought I was continuing my education. If she had her way, I would have dropped out of high school at sixteen and gotten a full-time job already." I bite my lower lip.

Ms. Levine clicks her tongue, and I look back at her. "Look, Eve. I want to speak to your mom. Maybe I can get through to her? Your mom has issues; we both know that. I really believe she only acts this way to you because she can't understand your potential. She's just trying to teach you how to survive. In your mom's opinion…now, this is just a guess, but I think in your mom's opinion, the books you read don't prepare you for actual life. But if she understood how much more is possible for you…"

I stare at Ms. Levine with hope, wanting so badly to believe her. Even though nothing in my entire life has ever pointed to the fact that my mom would support me, she's still my mother. Unfortunately, there's a part of me that wishes for her approval.

Instead of replying, I pick my pen back up. When we're finally done filling out the paperwork, she makes us some hot cappuccinos from her fancy Nespresso coffeemaker. "One day, I need to buy myself one of these," I tell her as I lift the mug up to my lips.

"Ready to write your last personal essay?" She turns her laptop around to face me. "You have to write about your biggest character flaw."

"Well, with so many to choose from…" We both chuckle.

"I'm going to run out and take care of some errands. Get comfortable. Write the essay. I'll review it when I get back in a few hours." She grabs her purse, letting herself out.

I go through a few drafts, feeling relief to get lost in the writing. I'm so involved in the work that somehow, hours pass without me getting up or needing to use the bathroom. By early evening when she returns, I have cramps in my legs, but also something I'm pleased with. She reads what I wrote and tears well in her eyes. "This is superb, Eve. Best one yet!"

Before the sun sets, I tell her goodbye and get on the downtown Six Train. This time though, Janelle is waiting at the stop when I get off. We walk together to the Blue Houses and I fill her in on the details of my day. She jumps up and down, thrilled about the possibility of my going to Columbia. "This way, you won't be far!"

CHAPTER 8

The following Sunday, I get to work early and open the shop. Even though it's tiny and rundown, I take pride in keeping the place immaculate. I turn on the lights and straighten the items around the store before removing the gun out of my bag and placing it close to my hand under the counter.

The gun has turned into a security blanket for me. I don't ever want to feel like my life is up for grabs; I need control over my safety. The reality is where I'm from, I need muscle to combat terror, and I intend on using whatever is available to keep my life intact.

I'm sipping my second coffee of the day while dusting the shelves when Angelo starts frantically banging on the front door to get my attention; he doesn't always remember to keep his keys on him. After pressing the buzzer to unlock the door, he walks straight up to me and puts his hands on my arms.

Alarm moves through me as I notice the sweat pouring down his face. "Listen, Eve. Something's come up." The lines in his forehead crease. "Antonio Borignone may be coming in here today with some other guys."

"Antonio? I thought you told me when I took this job I'd never have to see him." My distress has my heart thrashing. Of course, I know the mafia owns this shop, but I didn't think I'd actually have to deal with them. Coming face to face with one of the biggest mobsters in Manhattan is a nightmare I hoped never to see. I haven't seen Antonio in person, but his reputation is vicious. Guns, women, gambling, murder…the list goes on.

Seeing the agony on my face, Angelo continues, "Look. Antonio isn't all bad…" His tone is softer as his voice trails off. "He gives to charity—"

"Angelo," I snap. "Don't give me that. I don't want to be an accessory in his crazy mobster shit, and if he's coming in, it can't be good!"

He has the decency to look apologetic, opening his hands to me like a peace offering. "Look. He gave me the heads-up he has a lot of business to take care of and this shop is the place it's going to happen. Just continue doing what you normally do while you're here, and don't look at anyone too closely."

I would walk out right now, but I need the money badly. On top of it all, I love Angelo too much to ditch him. The only thing to do now is to get as much information as possible about what's about to go down. "Well, is he going to try and talk to me?" I manage to squeak out the words, trying not to let the fear take over my body.

He shrugs his shoulders in a questioning motion. "Look, I'm not part of the family. I'm just an associate. I have no clue what he's planning to say or not say to you. All I know is he's going to be coming in here with some of the crew, and they'll be using the basement. Typically, they don't all walk in together. They stagger themselves. Your job is to not look too closely at him or anyone else who comes in, okay? I don't want anyone to see your gorgeous face and get any ideas." I look at him incredulously, shocked he'd think such a thing.

"For fuck's sake, just do me a favor and keep your head down, okay? No eye contact. No speaking. Just look down." His no-nonsense attitude straightens me out and brings me back to earth.

I know Angelo cares about me and just wants to keep me safe. It's not as if he asked for this. "Okay, Angelo. I'll stay quiet and keep my head down."

"That's a good girl, doll," he replies, his tone softening. "Now, can I buy you a bagel or something?"

"Yes. Feel free to buy me breakfast for the next week." I say, trying to calm myself down. As he steps out of the shop, I take a novel out of my backpack. I'm getting to the good part when I hear the buzzer. Absentmindedly, I press the button to open the door, assuming Angelo is back with the food.

I lift my head happily, but freeze when I see an incredibly handsome man in a fitted navy suit walking inside. I gulp, praying this isn't Antonio. Whoever he is though, he's got a dominating presence and walks like a man of importance. He has black hair, sprinkled with some white at the temples. I take him to be a bit over six feet, with wide shoulders that taper into a narrow waist. When he steps up in front of me, I'm met with eyes so blue it's shocking. There's something about him that feels so familiar, but I can't put my finger on it.

He smiles casually, but his jaw is tight and the cold look in his eyes is at odds with his nonchalant smile.

"Can I help you?" I ask nervously, tucking my book away beneath the counter and putting my hand on the gun. The way he's looking at me has me shifting from one foot to the other. His handsomeness is quickly eclipsed by the fear he's putting out.

He slowly licks his lips. "I think you can. Where's Angelo?" He brings out a pack of cigarettes from his pocket and casually pulls one out. My heart starts to thump and eyes widen; this must be Antonio. I can feel it. There is no smoking in here. But there's no way in hell I'm about to tell this guy that.

He puts his cigarette into his full, pouty mouth. "You know who I am, sweetheart?" He's raising his eyebrows at me and again I'm struck with the feeling I've seen him before. He's staring at me while he lights up and inhales, and I can do nothing other than gulp while my internal alarm shrieks.

He blows the smoke out of his mouth and leans against the counter while I stare at him dumbly, unable to reply.

"You must be Irina's daughter, right?" He takes another inhale and smiles.

I try to manage words, but I end up stammering. "Uh, yeah." I attempt to keep my face straight as my panic builds.

"I see the resemblance, although you're a lot more beautiful than she is." His mouth widens in a half smile. "Look at you." He moves close to me, pushing an errant hair away from my face with his free hand, studying me. I can smell his cologne and can instantly tell it's expensive. I hold my breath, afraid to breathe anything of his into my body. I blink my eyes a few times and turn my gaze to the left, trying not to make any eye contact. Even though it doesn't feel sexual, his touch brings on a terrified buzz that's rising from my chest down into my toes.

He raises his eyebrows. "You're afraid of me. Good. Your mom tells me you're smart. She doesn't like it much." I drop my head and he bangs his hand down on the counter. "Look at me when I speak to you!" I jump at the sound of his voice, facing forward.

He chuckles. "That's better, sweetheart." His voice is lower now and somehow even more terrifying. "You want to go to college?" When I hear the word *college*, my mind focuses on my future. I straighten my back and grip my gun with all my strength, ready to do whatever I may need to do. Feeling the cool metal against my hand centers me. I have control. I can handle this.

"Yes. I'm going to go to college," I say with as much strength as I can muster.

"Hm, I see." He smirks. "You're strong and intelligent. Still blooming, though. Just gotta grow up some. It's basically impossible for a girl like you to get out of this life. You know that though."

I nod my head.

"If one of these shitty street gangs in your neighborhood got their hands on a pretty piece like you, it wouldn't go so well. Angelo tells me that you're a good girl. Still innocent. Always got your head in the books and helping Alex with his work."

I swallow, wondering if he's mentioning the street gangs because he knows something about Carlos. Every part of my body is freaking out right now. This is the man who has my mom and half of New York City wrapped around his pinky finger. He can order my death and burn my body without anyone noticing. Hell, even if they noticed, the cops would probably help dig my grave. Antonio's got everyone in his back pocket, and I'm nothing but a blip on his radar.

From the corner of my eye, I watch Angelo running back across the street. In some strange reaction, laughter bubbles up into my chest. I want to control it, but it breaks free, straight out of my lips. Antonio looks at me like I'm a lunatic as I'm cracking up, but there is no stopping it. The combination of Angelo running toward the shop while the most dangerous man in Manhattan stares me down has my wires crossed. I'm still laughing uncontrollably as I hold my finger on top of the buzzer, waiting for Angelo to open the door.

Angelo jumps inside, holding a plastic bag full of food. "Antonio, how are ya?" he asks gregariously, dropping the plastic bag on the counter and wiping the sweat from his face with the back of his hand. I blink as the laughter finally dies down and realize that my face is full of tears. Christ, Antonio must think I'm certifiable.

They shake their hands like old friends as I hiccup, trying to compose myself. I wipe my face dry with a tissue from the counter as Angelo slicks his hair back in a nervous gesture. "Go into the back, Antonio, everything should be comfortable for ya. Just text me if I can bring anything down." Antonio nods, not unkindly, and lets himself into the basement without a second glance backward.

When the door closes, Angelo makes eye contact with me, letting out a deep breath. "Good job, sweetheart. You've met the big boss. Just calm down now, all right? He won't hurt you. I wouldn't have left if I knew he was about to come. Now as the others come in, keep your head down. I'll do all the talking." I turn around and grab some paper towels that I use to wipe down the counter, handing some to Angelo. He nods in thanks and uses it to wipe the sweat off his temples.

I walk into the bathroom in the back, splashing some cold water on my face. Staring in the mirror and gipping the counter, I tell myself to relax. Okay, so I've met Antonio Borignone. It doesn't mean anything.

I step back to the front and one at a time, in intervals of twenty minutes, seven other men come into the shop. Each man is wearing a suit, but none of them are as good-looking and charismatic as Antonio.

Angelo comes over to the desk. "Listen. Why don't you head out early? Someone else is still on his way, but I don't want you to be here when he comes." He hands me a wad of cash with a wink. "A little extra for putting up with today, doll." I take it from him with a smile and grab my stuff to leave the shop, thankful to be away from the Borignones.

I stop at a small bodega and order a hot coffee while I read my book. I'm not in a rush to go home and it's not close to dark yet. At the very least, I want to turn my mind away from Antonio and jumping into the book world always helps me to relax.

A few hours later, I meander toward the bus stop. I'm about to sit on the bench when I see Vincent striding down the street. I stare at him dumbfounded, not sure what he's doing here. I'm frozen, with my mouth agape.

"Eve? Is that you?" He walks up to me, shock written all over his gorgeous face. His eyes widen as he takes me in, full lips quirking up in a surprised smile. He's wearing a fitted gray suit and looks sexier than any man has a right to look. My heart pounds.

"Yeah, um, I work nearby," I stutter out, pointing around the corner.

"Where?" he asks, brows furrowed in question.

I would bet money he's never heard of it. Vincent is the epitome of uberwealthy and finely educated. Trying to sound casual, I clear my throat. "Angelo's Pawn." I keep my head up after I tell him, not wanting him to see me as pathetic to work in a dive like that. I know that Angelo is amazing and the work is decent, but to a man like Vincent, it may seem like I work in a complete shithole.

Surprisingly, his eyes instantly widen when he hears the name, as if he knows the place and can't believe I work there. Before I can come to terms with the look on his face, he reins himself in. I'm left wondering if I just imagined the whole thing.

He pushes his hair back with his hands. "You heading home? I can drop you off."

The bus pulls up. My eyes flit between Vincent and the driver. Oh, who am I kidding? I've been dreaming of this moment for days and there's no way I'd let this moment pass me by.

"Okay," I tell him, biting back a smile. We walk a few blocks together in silence when I finally get the nerve to ask him what he's doing around here.

He pauses, thinking for a moment. "I train at a gym nearby." I want to ask which gym, but don't want to seem nosy.

We get to his car, a sleek black Range Rover. He opens the door for me and I jump in. It's impossible not to notice the beautiful leather seats and high-tech gadgets on the console. I let my fingers touch the buttery leather, trying not to freak out.

"Do you feel like eating?" he asks, buckling his belt.

I immediately remember how incredible the food was at the restaurant. Of course, my stomach chooses that moment to grumble.

"I take that as a yes?" He glances at my stomach as he puts the car in drive.

"Sure," I reply nervously, casually lifting one shoulder in a shrug. We pull up to a French restaurant with a black awning. From the outside, it looks incredibly fancy. My eyes scan my clothes and I realize that I'm seriously underdressed for a place like that. I'm in loose-fitting, low-rise jeans and a white T-shirt. I quickly pop down the visor and thankfully, see a mirror. Unfortunately though, the girl who gazes back at me is frizzy-haired and tired looking. A five-star dinner can't happen tonight.

"Uh, Vincent, I'm not so sure I can do something so extravagant." I gesture to my clothes.

My breath stops as his eyes take me in. "You're damn near perfect, Eve. But if you want, we can grab some pizza instead. I know a great place nearby."

I sigh in relief, trying not to blush at his compliment. "Yeah, let's do that." We park the car a few blocks over on the street and walk to Gino's Pizza on the corner. The bell chimes as we enter the restaurant. It's small and cozy, with red and white checkered floors and black tables. He tells me to take a seat in the back while he orders. I walk toward a table, choosing one near the window.

I sit and stare at Vincent as he checks his phone. Whatever he sees isn't making him happy; his forehead is creased, giving him a look of agitation. His turn is up to order and he lets go of whatever was bothering him, making small talk with the guys at the counter. They're so friendly as if they've known each other awhile.

He turns to me, catching me staring and mouths, "Hi." He stares at me openly, without any reservation; it lights me up inside. A few minutes later, Vincent walks over to the table, holding a large covered pizza box in his hands.

"That's all for us?" My eyes widen. There's no way we could eat all of that food!

He places it on the table and drops into the seat right next to me.

"I'm a growing boy, Eve," he jokes.

"Well, I'm starving, so thank you," I tell him appreciatively. I'm waiting for him to open it, but before he can, a booming voice sounds from the back.

"Yo, Vincent, you didn't tell me you were coming by!" A huge middle-aged man comes barreling out of the kitchen, wearing a white apron and smiling ear to ear. His accent is all Brooklyn.

Vincent stands to greet him. "Pauli, I miss you, man." They embrace each other warmly as if they're genuinely happy to see each other. Vincent is much taller, but Pauli looks heavier and undoubtedly solid looking.

Pauli looks at me, a pleased look on his smiling face. "And what's your name, darlin'? Always got the most gorgeous girl with ya, huh Vince?" I smile outwardly, but immediately feel slightly let down. How many girls does he bring here? Clearly, I'm not the first. I'm surprised by my reaction. I want

99

to be special to him; I want to be unlike the other girls before me. Because to me, Vincent is all I can see.

Vincent moves next to me, placing a hand on my shoulder. "Pauli, this is Eve. Eve, Pauli is an old friend of my family." I smile up at him, standing as I put my hand out to shake his. Before I know it, he swings around to my side of the table and hugs me to his chest. My eyes widen in surprise at his friendliness.

Pauli chuckles. "Damn, Vince. Sweet as hell, this one." His touch is kind, but still, I feel shy from the attention. I watch as Vincent's throat moves in a hard swallow. My reaction to his disapproval is to take my seat. Vincent lets out a half smile, and I feel relief. Something about him is just so dominant; I can't help myself but try to please him.

Pauli turns his attention back to Vincent. "So, how's life going?" He moves back around and drops himself into the chair across from mine.

Vincent takes his seat next to me, placing a possessive hand on my thigh. "You know how it is. Never a dull moment." The men chuckle together when we hear a group speaking Russian loudly. Vincent looks at them, his face deadly. I suck in a breath, unsure what just brought on this change.

"Aw, shit," Pauli says, bunching up a dishtowel in his fists.

"These guys been giving you trouble, Pauli?" Vincent asks. "I thought the Russians knew to stay out of your way." I sit still as he visibly hardens, his eyes impossibly darker.

I blink for a moment, looking between Vincent and Pauli, who seem to be engaging in a silent conversation. Vincent stands up from the table and stalks over to the group. They all seem to be talking for a second or two until the Russians run out of the pizzeria, practically tripping over their own feet in what looks like terror.

I eye Pauli nervously. When he sees the look on my face, he begins to laugh. "Oh shit, Vince," he calls out. "Got yourself an innocent girl, huh? Much better than that redhead." I'm taken aback by his comment, still not understanding what the hell is going on.

Vincent moves back to us, smirking. "All right, Pauli. Get the hell outta here; make some pizzas or something." They hug again before Pauli leaves.

"Come back anytime, sweetheart," he winks at me. "For you, pizza is always on the house." He leaves us and I'm left with questions.

"Vincent, w-what happened with those guys?"

"The Russians? They're always causing trouble around here. Just got them to move along."

"Yeah but—"

"Let's eat before this gets cold." I want to press him, insist that he can't just silence me. But with one look out the window, all thoughts of the Russians flee my head. It's almost dark, and I'm still not home.

"Shit," I say out loud, anxiety hitting me square in the chest. Noticing my nerves, he grabs my hand.

His face is full of concern. "What's wrong?"

I press my lips together. "I don't really like getting home when it's dark out." I feel a pounding headache starting up in the back of my skull. What if the Snakes are around? I'll have to find somewhere safe to wait until Janelle can come to me.

"I'm going to drive you home and walk you straight to your apartment door." His eyes are full of reassurance and understanding. "Nothing to be nervous about when you're with me, yeah?" He is confidence and strength. Rubbing his thumb across my knuckles, I'm immediately put at ease. I trust that when I'm with Vincent, no one will ever hurt me.

As he strokes my hand rhythmically, I let myself get lost in his dark eyes. They're gleaming, reminding me of the ocean at night—endless. He lets go of my hand and I feel immediately colder. He moves to open the pizza box, and I'm awakened from my trance.

He smiles. "Still hot." We eat together while he tells me about the best pizza spots he's ever been to.

"Last summer, I went to Capri for a few weeks. The food was incredible and the pizza was something else." He takes a huge bite.

I move in closer to him, wanting to hear more. "Who did you go with?"

"Remember Tom from the fight?"

"Mmhmm."

"Yeah. I went with him and…a few other friends." His eyes look down for a moment. "We took a flight to Naples and then a boat to Capri. It can get too touristy, but the beaches are insane and the food is probably some of the best in the world." He tucks a stray piece of my hair behind my ear, and I move closer to him.

I lick my lips, the motion bringing his gaze down to my mouth. "I've never even left New York," I tell him honestly. "I can't imagine what it must be like to travel so… freely."

"Never?" He seems surprised. "Not even to like, Jersey?"

I start to laugh and then click my tongue. "Not. Even. Jersey." I punctuate each word in a way that has him laughing. My tendency is to feel ashamed, but he isn't looking at me like I'm pathetic for never having traveled. Instead, he's looking at me in what feels like wonder. "You know, there are people in this world who don't just pick up and go whenever they feel like it." I raise my eyebrows at him.

"Yeah, yeah. But you're the type who'd love it. Maybe one day we—" He starts but immediately stops himself. Picking up a napkin to wipe his mouth, my chest warms with the words he didn't say.

"Yeah. One day, maybe." I sigh. "Anyway, as of now, I go lots of places. In books, of course." I wink.

"Cheapest way to travel, eh?" His eyes sparkle.

Our conversation picks up again and before I know it, I've eaten three slices and it's after eight o'clock. He stands to throw away the empty box and takes my hand to leave.

Arriving at the Blue Houses, I'm relieved to see that the elevator works. He brings me upstairs and walks me to my door, as promised.

"Thank you for dinner and for bringing me back," I tell him quietly.

"My pleasure, Eve." I wait a moment, wishing he'll kiss me. Instead, he looks at me with a satisfied smile on his face. He can tell what I'm waiting for, but for whatever reason, he's decided not to give it to me. I sure as hell won't ask for it if that's what he's waiting for.

I clear my throat. "All right. Well, bye, Vincent," I say in an exaggerated voice, waiting for him to go before I let myself inside my apartment.

"If you say bye, you gotta go inside before I leave," he tells me, as if everyone in the world knows this.

"No." I place my hands on my hips. "You walk away first. After you leave, I'll go inside." What the hell? I'm not backing down. It's not even that it matters who walks away first, but I'm tired of him always deciding everything.

His face turns to stone and I immediately take a step back. "Eve. Walk through your door." He points behind me. "I'm not leaving until I hear it click shut and until I know you are safely behind it." He crosses his arms in front of his chest, stance wide. His face is serious, but I'm not going to budge. Sure, he's huge and sexy and strong. But screw that! I'm not a docile idiot he can order around!

"No one is going to snatch me away from the door, Vincent. You go first!" My voice is laced with attitude and he raises his eyebrows at me in surprise, lips quirking up. "I refuse to do what you say. You think you can just push me into doing what you want like you probably do to everyone else? Wanna throw me out like you did those guys at the pizza shop?" I cock my head to the side. I don't usually give this kind of lip, but it feels freaking good.

He takes a step closer, crowding me. I step back, my hands pressing against the door. I'm technically trapped, yet surprisingly, unafraid. "When I tell you to do something—" his voice is gruff as he moves even closer "—you should listen to me, Eve." The way he says my name, like a warm caress, sends a flutter straight through me. Common sense is telling me that I should be afraid, but I want him so badly, I'm aching. Is it possible to be nervous and this turned on at the same time? Apparently, my body says *yes*.

Before I know it, he lifts me up in his arms, pulling me hard against him as my legs wrap around his waist. His lips move to mine as my hands grab his thick hair. We both moan as our lips lock. He pushes me against the door, his kiss demanding and controlling. I'm completely helpless, but God, it feels amazing. I want him to come inside my apartment, but there's no privacy. For all I know, my mom is home. I'm feeling frenzied as he puts his mouth on the side of my neck and sucks in deep. It feels so good that my mouth drops open and I gasp. I can't control the sounds coming out of my mouth as I feel his hot wet tongue on my skin. I pull his shirt up from his suit pants and with my shaking hands, manage to open a few buttons. I need to feel him. Oh. My. God. His chest is hot and taut over hard muscle. I move my hands upward and feel him tremor; I've never felt so powerful in my life. All thoughts disappear as he continues to kiss me like his life depends on it. He sucks on my tongue and my entire body bucks forward, asking for more.

I'm in a daze by the time he puts me down. I look him up and down, trying to commit to memory his sexy, rumpled appearance. "Forget the Bull. You're Batman." I put my fingers to my numb lips, giggling.

"Why Batman?" His eyes shine.

"Because you're like, underground fighter one second and all suited up the next. The duality, you know?" I cock my head to the side.

He shakes his head from side to side. "Baby, you have no idea how right you are. My entire life is duality. One foot in one world, one foot in another." I'm not sure what he's talking about, but the way he's staring at me has me wanting to jump back on top of him.

"How's it going?" I bite the side of my lip, trying not to smile.

He sighs. "It fuckin' sucks. But hopefully soon, I'll be able to simplify."

"Simplify?" I repeat, my voice full of question.

"Yeah. Simplify."

He leans against the doorway, legs crossed. He's clearly waiting for me to let myself in. With a sigh, I turn my body around and finally turn the key in the lock. Before I can step inside, he gently pushes me into my apartment and shuts the door on my face. I can hear him laugh and I mentally curse him. He always wins, damn it! I stand on my tiptoes to look through the peephole, watching as he leaves, a smile on his face.

When I go to the bathroom to shower up, I notice he's left a huge bruise low on my neck. What the hell? He marked me! I start smiling like a fool. Maybe I won, after all.

CHAPTER 9

It's three fifteen on Monday, and my mom just walked into Ms. Levine's classroom. Surprisingly enough, I haven't heard any yelling yet. I tried telling her earlier this week that meeting with Mom is pointless, but she insisted that maybe a different tactic would work. Hearing their voices increase in volume, I know I made a big mistake letting them meet.

Sitting on the floor of the empty hallway, I keep myself busy by reading the graffiti on some of the lockers. Apparently, Joaquin has a small dick and Chanel likes to suck it. Another locker is tagged with Snakes' symbol: a red circle with a capital *S* inside. My stomach does a slow churn as I stare. I try to turn my thoughts to Vincent, but there's no room for beauty in my mind right now.

When I hear Ms. Levine yell, I close my eyes and raise the hood of my black sweatshirt over my head. It's a men's hoodie and completely hides my shape, but I feel more comfortable having armor between my body and the world.

"Your daughter should go to college. Look at these scores! Her SATs are unbelievable. Don't you want her to go places other than *here*?"

"Ms. Levine," my mom screams, her voiced laced with aggression. I can only imagine her standing tall right now, getting all up in Ms. Levine's face. "How many fuckin' times do I have to tell you people? When she's done with high school in a few months, she's going to get a job like everyone else we know! Stop putting nonsense in her head! Do you think living is free? That I can just continue to support her while she studies?" I hear my mother's sarcastic laughter. "You don't know shit about our reality. If she's going to survive, she needs to thicken her skin. Not be deluded into thinking that there's a way out. There is no way out for her; this is her real life. You want to do her a favor? Toughen her up. Teach her some goddamn street smarts in that class of yours; don't I know she's got none of those!"

I hear Ms. Levine speaking, but can't make out her words.

"No!" my mom yells again. "You aren't listening!"

I expect the conversation to be over, but Ms. Levine continues. "That's the point! She doesn't have to live this life! Give her a chance to make something of herself one day!" Her voice pleads.

Not one ever to let someone else get the last word, my mom goes on. "My kid is staying where I am and where her sister is. Fuck this school. You think those rich people will accept a girl like her? I know people who tried to leave. Yeah, she's white. But she's poor and those rich assholes can smell poverty in seconds."

I hear the skid of a chair against the floor and not a moment later, my mom comes barreling out of the room. She stares down at me sitting on the floor, her face tight. I try to stand up, but she bends down and grips my hand like a vise, roughly pulling me off the floor. Her manicured nails pierce my skin as she tears us out of the building, high heels *clicking* at an amazing speed. We move through the metal detectors while the security guards are too busy checking out my mom's impressive cleavage to notice or care that she's on a rampage.

The bus pulls up to the stop at the same time we do, and we get on quickly, taking two seats in the back. Dread pools in my veins when I see the manic look in her eyes. This turned out worse than I imagined. I try to calm down and make myself invisible by putting the hood back on my head, but having my mom so physically close to me when I feel her mania on the rise makes it impossible to focus on anything other than fear.

We get off the bus and go inside our building. My mom walks straight to the elevator and presses the *up* button with a sharp red nail, but the light won't come on.

"Fuck!" she exclaims. "Of course, the shit box is dead again. Someone gotta get shot before anyone fixes anything 'round here."

I see the "storage" room next to the elevator and blink a few times, feeling lightheaded. I need to get out of here and into our apartment. She pulls her cell phone from her bag and turns on the flashlight as I open the heavy fireproof door for the two of us. We start up the steps. Her phone is raised above her head, casting a small spotlight in an otherwise dark stairwell. The lights in here have been dead for some time; it's like a black hole right now.

When we get to the fourth-floor landing, I open the stairwell door and start down the hallway for our apartment, hoping maybe she's mellowed out some since the conference. But before the thought can exit my brain, I feel her take hold of my shoulders from behind and turn me around to face her. She slaps me hard across the face, the smack echoing through my ears. My head swings to the side from the force, my long and dark ponytail whips around my face.

"Eve. How many times have I told you to stop showing off in school? Stop dreaming! You think you're better than me? Than all of us?" Even though I know there isn't any blood, it feels like the bones in my face have been shattered. My eyes fill with tears as I stare at her forehead. If I look into her eyes, she'll think I'm talking back, but if I don't look at her face, she may think I'm disrespectfully avoiding her stare.

"You need to learn how to toughen up. Do you hear me? This life is what you've been given. Reading books and going to college won't get you anywhere but dead!" She's yelling now, shaking me hard with both her hands. In her own sick way, she's just trying to get me to see something that I already know: I'm not suited to live this life. I know I'm different from my neighbors and it doesn't serve me well. I keep my head down and hide, hoping to just get through my days without getting hurt. My mom keeps trying to wake me up—thinking that if she pushes hard enough, I'll learn how to navigate the streets and save myself.

"You think I don't know about what happened with you and the Snakes? I heard about it from some girls at the club. You're lucky your sister is so well-liked in this building and she saved your ass. But one day, your luck will run out. You've got to *grow up*! You see this place? This is where you live. This is who you are. You'll never be more than this. If you read every book in the world, you'll still be you. A nobody." Her words sear my insides. "If you want to do something good for yourself, go be Carlos's girlfriend for a while. He'll eventually get over you and you can move on with your life. The more you resist, the worse it'll be when he finally catches you."

With those parting words, she turns from me and walks to our apartment door, opening it forcefully and slamming it shut behind her. I close my eyes, leaning against the corridor and sinking down until I'm crouched on the dirty floor in a daze. I put my hood back on my head and lean into it, letting the black cotton cover my eyes. Her words are sobering; the truth in them rattles around my head. I want to think about Vincent, but it's useless. A man like him has no business with a girl like me. It isn't until I hear someone nagging about the electric bill that I'm shaken out of my thoughts.

Picking myself up off the floor, I walk into my apartment and straight into my room. Closing the door behind me, I strip out of my clothes and put on a pair of old and worn sweats before crawling into my bed. I'm relieved to see it's only five o'clock. I love getting into bed early and reading the night away. I take the new book Ms. Levine recommended off my bedside table, and escape my life by entering someone else's.

When I finally doze off to sleep, I dream of Vincent. He's lying on a white sandy beach with a group of friends while I'm drifting in the ocean on a small red raft. I see him and call out, but no matter how loudly I yell, he doesn't see or hear me.

I wake with a start when I hear the front door open and close. Checking my bedside clock, I see it's two in the morning. My sister comes toward me in the dark. I can see her tiptoeing, trying not to make noise. "Hi Janelle," I croak, rubbing my eyes and wincing, feeling my face sting.

She turns on a small lamp in the corner of the room and lets out a gasp. "Holy shit, what happened to your face?" She flips on the rest of the lights, inspecting my cheek with her warm hands.

"Mom. She came to school today to talk to Ms. Levine and went berserk afterward."

Janelle goes to the kitchen and comes back with a pack of frozen peas, placing it gently on my face. She sits on my bed as I sit up. "Girl, you're gonna bruise from this. Je-sus she hit you good. That Ms. Levine. Always lookin' on the bright side…" She lets out a sigh, looking into my eyes sadly.

"Let me do your makeup tomorrow, okay? Keep this ice on your face as long as you can stand it." She turns away from me and walks into the bathroom. I press the cold bag to my face, shuddering from the sting. When I can't take it anymore, I close my eyes and curl back under the covers, letting my body relax into sleep. It's fitful.

I wake up the next morning in exhaustion, and my face is sore and bruised. Janelle tries to put some concealer and powder on me to take the discoloration away. When I look in the mirror, I see that it actually looks a lot better with the makeup. With no time to wash my hair, I put a black baseball hat on my head and jump onto the bus to get to school. I get off and walk directly to the English Department. When I see Ms. Levine sitting in her office, I walk inside and slam the door behind me.

I put my fists on her desk and lean my body forward, getting in her face like I've seen countless students do to intimidate teachers. I've never acted like this before, but my hurt has taken over.

"Don't say anything to my mom anymore. I'm never leaving this place, and I want you to pull my applications out!" The tears start to run down my face as she looks at me with sympathy. Fury takes hold, and I have an urge to smack the compassion off her face.

My hands shake. "My mom is doing this for my best interest, and in the best interest of my family. I have to stay here. I'm graduating in six months, and then I'm getting a job!" I yell.

She stands from her desk and closes the blinds, making sure none of the other teachers or students witness my outburst. She stands next to me in front of her desk, trying to take my hand. I ball them into fists, hating the feeling of her kindness.

She steps back, eyes gentle. "I know you, Eve. And I'm not pulling those applications. Do you hear me? I know you're scared. But one way or another I'm getting you out of this life. You deserve better," she pleads. "I see your face right now. You can't cover bruises like that with makeup and a hat. I made a bad judgment call bringing in your mother. I should have listened to you. Regardless, you're too smart for this," she states firmly. "I'm not giving up on you."

"I'm nothing. Stop trying to turn me into something. It's only making my life worse, can't you see that? All these promises, it's all bullshit. I don't know anyone who ever went to these fancy schools, except YOU. I wouldn't even know the first thing about doing well at a school like that…and…this—" I glance around the shoddy room "—is who I am." My voice breaks off at the end.

She shakes her head woefully, stepping closer to me again. "We'll hear back from colleges shortly. I'm still crossing my fingers that you can start somewhere in June. Just hang in there a little while longer, Eve." She finally takes my hand, and I let her. "I'm not leaving you alone, all right? Don't be afraid." Her eyes show concern, and I know she's doing this because she cares, but I'm too hurt to accept it. When the first bell rings, I walk out of the room, no longer having the energy to speak.

I go to my first period math class and zone out, telling myself I need to calm down and let the applications stay in motion. Ms. Levine is right. I can't just give up after all I've put into this. I look out the window and watch as a delivery truck parks illegally to bring crates into one of the bodegas. While he's away, three kids jump into the back of the truck and run out with their hands full of loot. Only a few minutes after that, the cops come and give the truck a ticket for double-parking. I'm living in Gangland.

JESSICA RUBEN

CHAPTER 10

The next morning, Janelle wakes me up by vaulting into my bed. The box spring and mattress is so old that I immediately bounce up.

"Today is gonna be a great day!" She hugs my exhausted body to her chest, lifting me like a ragdoll. "It's the freakin' weekend, baby, I'm about to have me some fun..." she sings, quoting "Ignition" by R. Kelly.

I rub my face, my voice coming out in a rasp. "Ugh, get off me, or at least wait until I've had my coffee." I get up, dragging my body to the bathroom. How Janelle has this energy in the morning, I'll never understand.

After washing up, I walk into our tiny kitchen to put the coffee on. I take out a pan and put it on the stove. I take out eggs and some milk, and immediately scramble them together. I don't cook anything fancy, but Janelle always tells me I've got a gift in the kitchen.

I put some toast in the oven and when it's all ready, call for my mom and Janelle. My mom lazily walks to our table with a short pink silk robe wrapped around her tall frame. She sits casually and waits for me to serve her.

I put the full plate in front of her, and she tenses. "Where's the butter and jam?" Her tone raises my guard. I quickly open the refrigerator, taking out what she needs and placing it on the table. Moving to the sink, I immediately begin to wash the pan I've already used, making sure to give her a show as to how diligently I clean. My mom will never lift a finger to maintain the apartment, but expects it to be spotless nonetheless; she has an obsession with cleanliness—and as far back as I can remember, always has. The sight of a mess really sets her off, so I do my absolute best to keep things organized at all times. While it's annoying to be constantly scrubbing, the stress of keeping things perfectly tidy is nothing compared to her wrath if things aren't up to her standard. I continue to scrub the dishes as my mind wanders back.

***

It's midnight. I'm officially thirteen years old. Mom barges through the door, unable to stand up straight. Janelle had just paused the show we were watching to wish me a happy birthday. We're in an embrace when she speaks.

"What the hell is this shit?" Her voice is low and gritty as she stares at us in the darkness.

"Mom?" Janelle asks, sitting up from the couch as my mom pulls off her patent-leather, sky-high platforms, dropping them to the floor. They clatter like dead weight onto the ground. We haven't seen her in over two weeks.

"What are you girls doing awake?" I feel goosebumps rise on my arms, and I pull the blanket tighter around me.

Janelle clears her throat. "Mom, we were just having fun…it's—"

"Having fun? I work hard for you girls!" She comes to the side of the couch, grabbing my arm and forcing me to stand.

"You like to stay up late? You're a little loser, you know that?" She cackles like she's never heard anything funnier. "I think you'll make a great housekeeper one day, Eve. Tonight, you better clean this shithole until it's sparkling." She flips the lights on, temporarily blinding us. "I'm waiting." A dark smile settles on her face.

My mother watches me wash every inch of the apartment until the sun rises.

***

I finally blink the memory away, realizing I've been scrubbing for way longer than necessary. I hear her voice over the running water. "So, how are you?" I shut off the faucet and turn toward my mother as she takes a long sip from her coffee mug, looking more tired and worn out than usual. It's a rarity that she asks how I am, and her question catches me off guard.

"I'm good, Mom," I say hesitantly, drying off the pan with a dish towel. I take a seat at the table across from her, wondering if she'll be decent this morning.

She hums. "You look good." She stares at me from the tip of my toes all the way up to my face. "You're beautiful?" It comes out more like a question than a statement.

I shrug, not replying. I'm not sure what she wants to hear and would rather stay silent than say something that may incite her. Somehow, she always manages to take my kindness as arrogance.

"You're still working at Angelo's, right?"

"Yeah, I am. It's still cool."

"Don't embarrass me while you're there," she snaps. My mom is forever trying to stay in the good graces of the family, and she'd probably kill me if I ever did anything to jeopardize her relationship. The Borignones are so powerful; I'd never—in my right mind—do anything that could even be potentially construed as messing with them.

She glances around the kitchen, her eyes skittish. "You need to clean this place better, Eve. I can see dust in all the corners. Can't you see it?" Her voice accuses.

I gather myself before replying. "I'll make sure to go over it again today." I try to speak with as much decency as I can muster; any trace of an attitude is a surefire way to get her angry.

"I'm taking a nap. When I wake up, I don't want to see this disgusting mess."

"Yes," I reply calmly.

Janelle walks in, smiling happily. My mom's gaze turns to my sister. When she's in these moods, anyone in her path is going to get run over. "Why do you look so happy, Janelle?" Her eyes move from Janelle to me, completely distrustful. Anxiety fills me. She's rising.

Janelle's voice is scratchy as she starts. "It's nice out and I have a full day of clients. Cha-ching!" My mom huffs as I bite my cheek, trying not to laugh.

For whatever reason, my mom never hurts Janelle in the way she does me. I'll never understand it. Not that I'd ever wish Janelle to feel how I'm feeling, but I just wish I knew why I'm always the one singled out.

My mom's face turns to ice, her eyes shrinking into slits. She's obsessively touching her bleached-blond hair, pushing the strands back from her face over and over again. Janelle and I watch as her mood morphs. She stands abruptly, leaving her dirty dish on the table for me to clear and wash. I take a breath of relief when she finally slams her bedroom door, retreating into her cave. Janelle brings her coffee back to our room, leaving me alone in the kitchen.

Sitting by myself, I feel totally relieved. Grabbing my cell off the counter, I scroll through the *Post* headlines while enjoying my eggs and hot coffee. When I'm done, I wash all of the dishes by hand and put them away neatly in the cabinets where they belong. I step into my room, dropping my body on my unmade bed and wishing I could see Vincent again. I only have a few hours before I need to get to work, and I don't want to waste any more time on anything other than him. I curl under my covers, shutting my eyes and trying to replay both of our times together for what feels like the trillionth time, when Janelle drops onto my bed, making me bounce up and shaking me out of my reverie. "So, you never told me about what happened with the hot guy you met from the fight." Her smile is all-knowing, and I flush inside.

I open my mouth, ready to spill every detail, but quickly shut it. I don't want to tell her anything about Vincent. The whole experience was so new and incredible, I'm afraid if I tell her that it will become less mine somehow. Like once I discuss it, it'll be out in the universe—and I just want to keep it close to my heart. Who knows if I'll ever have something like that again. I got lucky twice, and something tells me a third time isn't in the cards.

Yes, I felt his want for me, but it was also more than that. He looked at me as if I'm someone worth knowing. He didn't see me like an uppity bookworm. And he didn't look at me like a poverty-stricken girl to pity, either. For some reason, he just seemed to actually like me. The real me. The me I almost never let anyone see. And God, I liked him. Almost too much.

"Nothing…" I say hesitantly, my eyes darting down for a moment while heat rises into my cheeks. She notices my blush and rolls her eyes.

"Wait," she asks me nervously. "You didn't have sex, right?"

My eyes widen with surprise and I laugh. "No! Absolutely not. We just made out and like, some other stuff…"

"Some other stuff?" She immediately sits up, wanting to know every detail.

"Yeah, like, I don't know. We made out. He touched me…uh, a little." I take a nervous breath. "I kind of had my first…you know..."

Her eyebrows rise up as she turns to me, smiling with surprise and shock. "Je-sus, Eve. Orgasm? If you can't say *orgasm*, God won't ever let you have one again. You know this rule, right? If you want it, you need to be mature enough to say it!" She's laughing hard, practically doubling over.

I'm so embarrassed I cover my face with the pillow. When I finally move it away to look back up at her, her eyes are sparkling with excitement.

"Eve. I'm seriously dying right now. God knows you're old enough. I need details! Did the guy have a huge dick? How was his tongue?" She raises her eyebrows up and down and I quickly bring the pillow over my head for a second time. "Well?" she asks expectantly, moving it away from my face.

"Janelle…it was…" All I can do is let out a heavy sigh, focusing my gaze on the ceiling. She lays back down next to me. "I know. When it's like that… it's everything."

Words just can't describe it. Instead of pressing me for more information, she throws her leg over mine and pulls me close to her. Janelle understands I'm not ready to talk, and she gives me the space I need. God, I love her.

"I'm so happy for you right now, Eve. I feel like my heart is about to burst. Whenever you're ready to talk, I'm here."

I let out a *hum* in response. I finally shut my eyes again, and he's all I see.

CHAPTER 11

The following weeks pass in a blur of school during the week and Angelo's on the weekends. I haven't heard from Vincent at all, but I'm too nervous to reach out to him. If he wanted to talk to me, he would have taken my number, right? Regardless, our times together are still on repeat through my head.

I grab my bag to leave Angelo's and type in the numbers for the alarm. I step outside and zip up my light jacket. It's going to be a cold winter for sure.

Shutting the door behind me, I pause when I see who's waiting out front. Vincent is casually leaning against his car, looking down at his phone. I stand there for a moment in wonder. Is he here for... me?

He glances up, dark eyes drinking me in as if I'm the first good thing he's seen in quite some time. I tentatively walk up to him, but he doesn't let my shyness dictate the moment. Instead, he takes my hand and pulls me flush against him, swallowing me up in a warm bear hug. I let out a sigh as I melt into his warmth. He smells so good. Part of me wants to ask him where he's been. But the bigger part of me is so deliriously happy, I can do nothing other than gush at the fact that he's here.

JESSICA RUBEN

He finally lets me go and wordlessly opens the car door, inviting me inside. I hop in and buckle up as Vincent shuts the door behind me. The car is so warm compared to the cold temperatures outside right now. He takes his seat, immediately grabbing my hand and smiling as if we were just together yesterday.

"How are you?" he asks, his voice full of gentleness.

"I'm great!" I tell him overenthusiastically. He chuckles at my excitement. "So, where are we going?" The happiness pulses through my veins; I can't contain it!

"I thought maybe we'd go to Wolman Rink in Central Park. Have you ever been skating?"

My smile stretches from ear to ear. "Oh, I've always wanted to do that!" I stop myself before I tell him that I used to dream of being a figure skater, even though I've technically never been on ice. I've skated lots of times in my mind though, so it's sort of like the real thing, right? I mean, how hard can it actually be?

He winks. "I guess I'll have to show you how." I'm staring out the window, daydreaming about how he'll hold me close to his body as we skate, hand in hand. It will be so romantic.

We pull into a parking garage near Central Park on Sixth Avenue. Vincent tells me to wait as he steps out of the car, throwing his keys to the valet before coming around and opening my door.

"Do you know him?" I ask, turning my head for a moment to get a look at the attendant. Maybe that's the normal way people treat car attendants, how should I know? From what I see about Vincent, he lives in a world that's totally foreign to me.

"Nah. But I know the owner of the garage, so most of the guys who work there know me." He's so nonchalant, walking forward like he's the master of his universe.

We walk through Central Park from the Fifty-Ninth Street entrance. Walking down a small hill toward the rink, the first thing I notice is how packed it is with people of all ages. I'm looking around in awe of the entire place with the city skyline as the background, while Vincent pays the admission fee and skate rental. We walk together into the pavilion when what feels like a million kids run past us. I grab Vincent, trying not to get mowed down. He laughs as I cling to him for dear life.

They finally leave the vicinity and I shake my head. "Kids these days, huh?" He laughs harder, and I join him.

People sip hot chocolates and coffees while munching on churros and soft pretzels. Vincent asks me for my sneakers and I pull them off, handing them to him. He gives the rental guy my shoes, who quickly goes to the back and returns with skates in my size.

"What about yours?" I ask curiously as we walk away.

"I've got my own pair of hockey skates with me." I finally notice that he's got a black sports bag with him, and I roll my eyes.

"Next thing you're going to tell me is that you were about to go pro with the NHL or something."

"Hah! You think I'm that amazing, do you?"

"Nope. But you definitely think you are," I quip, smiling.

"I'm not too bad, am I?" He gives me a sly grin and I try not to melt in a puddle on the floor.

"So, when did you learn to skate?" I ask, trying to get as much information out of him as possible.

"I used to take lessons when I was a kid. I showed a lot of promise, but I preferred football." His eyes gleam.

"Really? That's so cool." My heart flutters. "So, how did the fighting start?"

"Well, martial arts has always been important to my father. It started out simply enough, we'd go together and learn. A bonding thing, I guess. But over time I got really good and started sparring with my coaches. They encouraged me to fight." he shrugs.

"Your parents know about it?" I ask suspiciously. I simply can't imagine any normal or decent parent encouraging their kid to brawl in the underground.

"My dad hates it," he replies coolly, finishing with his skates.

I finish tying mine, but I'm unsure if I pulled my laces tight enough. Without a word, he drops down on one knee in front of me, tightening them. I smile, an idea taking shape in my head. "No, I will not marry you, Vincent," I'm loud, garnering the attention of some people around us. He starts to snicker, shaking his head at me.

"Please, Eve," he replies loudly. "You're the most intelligent, kind, and beautiful woman on earth. Say *yes*! Don't keep denying me!" I do my best not to die of embarrassment as more people turn toward us. I know I started it, but I didn't think he'd continue. "How many times do I have to ask? Marry me! Be my wife! Be the mother of my children," he pleads.

I huff, looking left and right and pressing my lips together in a firm line. "Fine. You've worn me down. I'll do it."

Some people cheer as he stands up, wrapping me into his arms. We rub our noses together in a cheesy but oh-so-sweet gesture, while my insides melt. I have to ask myself, who am I right now? Vincent brings out a side to me that I never knew existed.

When he finally pulls back, there's an undeniable electrical current between us, and I can feel it down into my toes.

"All right, wife." He winks. "Let's finish putting these on." He moves back down to my feet and finishes lacing up my skates, pulling the strings tightly. We stand up together, ready to get on the ice. Before we can leave, he pulls out a white hat, scarf, and gloves from his bag. He slides the hat on me and I blink hard in utter confusion as soft warmth blankets my head.

"I know I didn't tell you we were coming here, and I didn't want you to be cold."

"You, b-brought this? For me?" My mouth literally drops open when I realize what he's done.

"Yeah," he replies easily, draping the scarf around my neck and tying it closed. Lifting each of my hands, he slides the gloves on one at a time. "There," he says, looking into my eyes. "Just right."

I'm totally struck dumb. Whatever he got me must be made from the softest material I've ever felt in my life. I turn over the tag from one glove and see it says 100% CASHMERE. Holy crap! I want to thank him, but I can barely muster the words.

"Uh, Vincent, I hope you kept the receipt—"

He lets out a chuckle. "Eve, it's for you. Keep them."

"No way. I can't keep something like this…" I shake my head vehemently.

He looks at me with confusion on his face, as if he can't imagine a girl saying *no* to a gift. "Look. I brought you here. I passed by Bloomingdales today and wanted to make sure you wouldn't freeze. It's my treat, okay? They're yours."

I wait a few moments, not sure what the protocol is for this. I can't even imagine what this gift must have cost. "Okay," I finally tell him, swallowing hard.

"Good. Now stay warm and try not to fall on your ass. Let me just put this in the back with your shoes." He gestures to his bag and I watch him walk away. I already feel much warmer, and I vow to take the best possible care of my new accessories.

He comes back to me and we start to walk toward the rink. I find myself losing balance and luckily, he grabs my waist, letting me lean into him. It's harder to stay steady on these skates than I originally thought.

When we finally get onto the ice, it's nothing like I imagined it would be. For starters, I don't feel graceful; I feel completely and utterly idiotic and clumsy. I try to move, but every time I slide my skates forward, I feel myself falling backward. Vincent takes hold of me as I cling to the wall for dear life.

"Okay, Tara Lipinski," he tells me jokingly. "Just stop a moment." I want to glare at him, but as I turn my head, my skates skid forward and backward again. I let out a huff as I grab the wall, realizing this is real life, not the fantasy. Little girls are gliding past me—twirling like swans—while I'm trying not to collapse to my death onto the cold and hard ice. Vincent keeps trying to stabilize me, but I can't stop myself from moving.

"Stop moving, Eve!" he stresses. I can tell from the tone of his voice that he's doing his best not to laugh his ass off at me.

"I'm trying, Vincent. But it's ice for God's sake!" I'm irritated by this turn of events. I was supposed to be naturally amazing at this and instead, I'm a failure.

"Watch your mouth," he whispers. "There are kids around."

I huff and try to stop my legs from falling out underneath me. I look up when I see someone ahead of me wipe out, landing on his ass. "Oh shit,

Vincent! Did you see that guy?" Vincent throws his huge arms around me, securing my body to his.

"Just focus on your breathing," he tells me soothingly. I let myself follow his order, and before I know it, I feel myself calm. "There we go, Eve."

Somehow, the breathing really does work. "Okay, I think I can stand now."

Vincent gently lets go of me and I stand up tall, without hanging onto the wall. I hold myself like a statue while he moves behind me, carting me around the ice with complete grace. For a man so huge and strong, it's amazing how he's able to be so agile. After the fifth turn around the rink, I feel comfortable enough to lift my arms out to my sides. "I'm flying!" I yell, giggling, turning my head to glance at him. Have I ever been this happy in my life? I don't think so.

After we've gone around the rink what seems like dozens of times, he pulls us back over to the side, turning my body to face him. I grab his waist, so I don't collapse, and look up into his eyes. "Oh my God, Vincent! That was the best!"

"Well, I'll give you an *A* for enthusiasm, that's for sure." The look on his face is all play.

I purse my lips. "Oh, come on! Once I got the hang of it—"

"The hang of it?" He squints his eyes and holds back a smile. "You mean, the hang of staying still while I carted your tiny ass around?"

"Yes! Exactly!" He pulls me into his hard stomach and I breathe him in, feeling his body move with a laugh. It just feels so undeniably right.

He pulls me back a bit, still holding me securely. "I brought us some food. Let's go back inside." He kisses the top of my head. Helping me off the ice, he pauses for a moment as I turn my face up to his again. His skin is warm from the exertion; eyes so dark and glassy they're almost black. I'm not sure where his parents are from, but I'd bet his ancestry is something unique. I try to study each of his features, wondering what combination of ethnicity may have given him these incredible looks.

"You like to stare, huh? I hope you like what you see." His smile stops my heart.

"I'm just wondering where your parents or grandparents are from."

"My father is originally from Italy and my mother was Native American," he easily replies.

Did he say, *was*? I would bring it up, but I don't want to spoil the happiness we've got going on right now. "Oh my God," I say out loud, smiling. "I can actually totally see that. The wideness of your cheekbones and the slight slant in your eyes. It's like nothing else."

He chuckles. "And what about you?"

"My mom is Russian. She tells me my father was from Brazil."

"Mmm," he says, nodding his head in understanding.

"What do you mean, 'mmm?'" I ask.

"Just that you're sexy as hell, that's what." I flush from his blunt compliment, immediately dropping my head. He's so forward and confident, it's disarming.

"Okay, my gold medalist. Let's go inside." He drapes his arm over my shoulders and I do my best not to lean on him as we walk. He abruptly stops, seemingly annoyed. "I've had enough of this wobbly walking. I'm afraid you're gonna fall."

"Well, what exactly do you want me to—" I'm cut off when he lifts me in the air and throws me over his massive shoulder. I want to protest, but I can't stop laughing; all the blood rushes down into my head. We get inside and he places me down at a table in the back corner with a gentleness that's completely at odds with his tough demeanor. I look around for a moment; our table is completely hidden behind a beam. Did he bring us here on purpose?

He unties my skates, pulling them off my feet. I feel instant relief as I wiggle my toes around in freedom. "Feels so good to take these off!" I exclaim.

Vincent pulls off his own skates. "It does, huh?" I nod my head in reply. I look down and notice how massive his feet are. I swallow hard, wondering if that old saying is true. Big feet, big…

"Let me take your skates up." He picks them up off the floor, walking back to the rental desk. A few minutes later, he brings my shoes back along with his gym bag.

Unzipping his bag, he pulls out bottles of water, four huge sandwiches, and two colorful-looking salads along with napkins and plates. I'm looking at all the food with wide eyes. He gets up again and walks over to the snack counter, bringing us back two large cups filled with ice.

I sit on the edge of the table and watch while he finishes setting everything up. I'm not used to being taken care of like this. He opens up the sandwiches, each overstuffed with meat and vegetables and cut in half. I can't wipe the grin off my face when I see all that he's done.

"You're a perfectionist, huh?" He places the food on the table in perfect symmetry and with a neatness I'm shocked he possesses. "I can't believe you did all this."

"The food here sucks, and I thought you'd like something else." He smiles casually, as if bringing food this amazing is not a big deal. To me though, it's everything. And it's not just the food. It's the thought. It's everything. It's him.

He looks down at me as something dark and filled with promise moves through his eyes. I swallow hard, the smile from moments ago wiped off my face. He's looking at me so intensely that I feel my breath quickening.

He picks up a sandwich and hands it to me, breaking our heat. "You'll like this," he says gruffly. I close my eyes and take a bite.

"Mm, it's delicious." And I'm not bluffing. It may be the best sandwich I've ever had. I open my eyes to see him watching me intently, his gaze moving from my eyes down to my lips and back up again.

"It's from Eataly."

"Oh, I've always wanted to go there—" I want to continue, but stop myself. Not that he doesn't already know, but girls like me don't get to eat at fancy restaurants with even fancier chefs. I can't stand the thought of him seeing me as lacking or even worse, pitying me. Thoughts about my poverty disappear though, as he continues to gaze at my mouth as I chew. I swallow my food as heat finds its way into my lower belly. He picks up his own sandwich and takes a gigantic bite.

For some time, we do nothing but eat and stare at each other. We're quiet, but the silence is completely loaded. It's weird how these things don't take prior experience to understand; something inside me, on a basic and carnal level, knows what's happening. Our eyes, full of energy, say everything.

My eyes: "God, you're gorgeous. Sexy. Brilliant. I love this."

Vincent's eyes: "I'm so happy you're here with me."

Some of his hair is messy on his forehead and I put my sandwich down, leaning forward to brush it off to the side. His look softens and I wonder for a moment if he had a mom who took care of him—if she used to pack him lunch and make him breakfast and dinner, if she tucked him in bed at night, reading stories. Did Vincent have his parents' bed to run to in the middle of the night if he ever had a bad dream? Even though he seems to have it all, something is telling me that his life may not be all roses. I want to ask him, but feel shy.

I take my last bites of the sandwich when I start to consider getting some sauce on my cheek just so we can have one of those movie moments where he wipes it off and kisses me. But as I squeeze the remainder of the sandwich in attempt to get the sauce on my face, I screw it up and somehow end up getting mayo on my pants.

"Shit!" I gasp, clicking my tongue and grabbing a napkin.

He starts to laugh and I quickly try to explain. "I didn't realize that the sandwich would squirt from just a small squeeze! I mean, shouldn't it take more than that?" His eyes seemingly widen with disbelief at my comment, and he starts cracking up. I'm not sure what's so funny about what I said, but something in the way he's laughing tells me he's laughing at me, not with me. His laughter is intensifying as I get redder and there is nothing else to do but hide my face with my hands.

When I realize he isn't planning to stop his laughter, I lift my hands off my face and hit him on the shoulder.

"Oh, shut it. Stop!" I feel so juvenile. My face is probably the color of a beet right now. "Stop laughing at me, Vincent!"

"I can't help it. You're so damn sweet..." He drags me onto his lap and I put my head into the crook of his neck. I feel his body shake with the remnants of his laughter and I take a sharp breath. All of a sudden, I realize I may have just found the greatest spot of all time. I nuzzle into his neck, inhaling his scent. I hope he doesn't think I'm creepy right now, but the truth is that I couldn't stop myself even if I wanted to. I want to crawl inside this man and never leave. For all his hugeness, we manage to fit so well. He finally stops laughing and brings his arms around me, pulling me flush against his chest and holding me firmly. I guess he likes this too. I receive confirmation when I feel him hardening under me. I pause. Slowly, I pull my head back.

Some young kids start nagging their mom about wanting churros, but it all becomes background noise as our lips connect. It's slow at first. Gentle lips and warm tongues. But the moment his hands go beneath my ass, he presses me down into his erection and all common sense flees my brain.

"Fuck." His voice is a growl and my eyes shut, the feelings overwhelming me.

Blood pools down low as he rubs me rhythmically against him. I move over a little to the left and let out a moan into his neck; he's hitting that spot. "Vincent..." I say into his skin. I can't even be bothered to realize where I am or what I'm doing. All I can do is grip onto his huge shoulders as he presses me down harder and harder. I feel myself start to sweat and I welcome it; the heat is devouring me from the inside out.

I lift my head for a moment and look into his eyes when he stops. When I realize he isn't going to continue, I exclaim, "What? No!"

He chuckles as he gently moves his hands from my back to my shoulders and takes a breath, turning me around so I'm sitting back on the bench beside him. "Later, okay? Here isn't the place for you." His eyes are filled with promise, but somehow, I'm left with this hollow and desperate feeling.

My body finally starts to wind down and I plunge my plastic fork into the salad, internally stressing about what is going on. And anyway, why did it take him so long to reach me? When we're together, I feel like we've got something more than just attraction. It's deep; I can feel it. But he disappears. And then he's back. I'm having emotional whiplash and frankly, I'm angry. I should have been pissed at him when he picked me up, but I was too overwhelmed by the emotions he brings out in me. He's too gorgeous. Too big. Too smart. Too everything!

I decide I may as well just get out with it and ask him. I turn my head to the side to get his attention, my anger fueling my tongue. "Vincent?" My voice comes out angrier than I intended. He looks into my eyes and smirks, as if he knows already what I'm going to say.

"Yeah, babe?"

I turn my body around so that instead of being side by side, I'm facing him. "What are we?"

"Hm. I think I'm a man, and you're a woman..." He starts to joke.

"Come on. I'm serious. What's happening here?" I gesture my hands between the two of us.

He takes a few moments before answering. "We're friends." His eyes are saying we're more, but his words obviously differ.

I startle for a moment and want to disagree with him. "But—"

He turns to face me. "I live a very complicated life, Eve." His eyes bore into mine as if he really wants me to hear what he's saying.

"Are you... with other girls?" I ask, my stomach sinking with dread.

He sighs but keeps his head up. "Let's start like this for now, okay? Let's just be friends." It seems to pain him to use the word, but it sure as hell feels like I've been knifed.

I try to silently communicate with my eyes how much I want him to be mine, but my chest pounds with feelings of inadequacy. I don't have the guts to tell him so.

Tears start to well in my eyes as I remember the mention of a redhead, but I swallow down my pain and try to keep my emotions in check. Why doesn't he want me? He watches as confusion and hurt cross my face. He looks as if he's about to say more, but he stops. Vincent has the self-control of a saint; if he chooses not to speak, nothing will leave his lips.

The truth is, I know why he doesn't want a girl like me. I'm a nobody. I'm a poor girl from the ghetto. What would a man like him want with someone like me? The answer is that he wouldn't.

133

He touches my shoulder. "No." He shakes his head. "I see what you're thinking, and I don't like it. There's a lot you don't know about me. Let's just finish eating, okay? We're cool. We're here right now. Let's be in the moment." He turns back around to face the table, essentially dismissing me.

"So tell me. Tell me what I don't know," I ask him desperately.

I wait, but he doesn't say a word. Finally, I turn myself back and finish my salad quietly. I'm not good enough, but this shouldn't be a surprise. My mom's words come back and hit me in the chest. I'm nothing. I look down at my shoes and feel the tears welling up again. He knows how poor I am, and probably sees me as nothing more than a toy to pass the time with. I try not to cry as I eat my salad. My mind is moving so quickly, I barely know what it tastes like.

When he finally brings me back to my front door, my shame is raging. I want to cry and scream at the top of my lungs. I wish he didn't drop me off here; it's nothing but a reminder to him of who I am and where I come from. But at the same time, I can't just waltz back home at this time of night. It's not safe, and it's undeniable that with him, I'm secure.

He leans against my shitty white doorframe. I want to ask him if I'll see him again, but I know that any words that come out of my mouth right now will sound desperate. He checks his phone and his face turns to agitation. I open my apartment door and let myself inside. Before closing it, I turn back around, thanking him again.

He puts his hand on my hips, bringing me closer to his body. I look down at the floor and back up to his face.

"Eve," he says, shaking his head. "Thank YOU for coming with ME. You're too sweet for a man like me. Too good. I've got more going on than you can imagine...but trust me, what I've got going on is not about you. You're perfect." I want to believe him. Hell, I'm begging inside for him to elaborate.

But he doesn't. On one hand, he sounds so genuine…and the scarf and gloves and hat…and the food! The connection we have seems undeniable. But then again, it feels as if he's breaking up with me. I've never been broken up with, but if it feels like my heart is being ripped out, I guess this qualifies.

I shrug my shoulder sadly, and for a brief moment, I think I see regret pass through his eyes. "I guess I'll see you soon, Vincent." I stare up into his face one more time and see so much pain pass through. He sighs, looking up at the ceiling and back down at me.

Moments pass and he's still silent. Somehow, I get the nerve to turn away from him, shutting the door behind me. I hear his heavy steps as he leaves, and I do my best not to cry.

CHAPTER 12

A month passes, and Vincent feels like a distant memory. I never discussed him with Janelle, and so in the daytime, it's almost like what happened between us didn't even occur. But every single night, he's the only thing I can see, smell, and taste.

Missing him began as an acute ache, and slowly filtered into the rest of my body. Ever since he disappeared, I feel like I'm always missing something. I leave home and feel it in my chest—it's not a sweater; it's not my phone or my wallet; it's HIM. He managed to fill a part of me I didn't even know was empty. And now that he's gone, I feel the hole gaping inside my chest.

This morning, Janelle and I are sitting together for breakfast before we head off to work. She sits across from me while I sip my coffee and read the newspaper. She looks nervous, so I drop my paper and ask her point blank. "What's up, Janelle? You look like you're going to freak out."

"Carlos is out," she says in a rush. I look at her face, feeling my stomach sink. She's playing with the hem of her shirt and glances at me nervously. Finally, her gray-blue eyes bore into mine, and I know that she's gearing up to tell me some serious shit.

With trembling hands, I put down my coffee mug. "Tell me."

"Yeah. Well, I heard he made bail—" She stops, clearing her throat. "I also heard that he's, um, angrier than usual." She stands, bringing the rest of the carafe of coffee to the table and pouring more into my cup.

I lick my dry lips. "What do you mean?"

She moves to the edge of her seat, pushing sugar my way. "Well, I was on the stoop yesterday. It was my day off. I was hanging out with everyone and listening to Mr. Samson talk about a new jazz club that recently opened up in Harlem. We were all getting high with someone's hash, shooting the shit—"

"And?" I raise my eyebrows, waiting for her to get to the point.

"Juan came over, and sat with me." She slightly shifts her head to the side and presses her lips together. "Well, he told me that Carlos is out now. And, he's been talking shit all over town that he and you have some unfinished business. Juan wanted to tell me because he's scared for you. I know he's an annoying little shit, but after he heard..." her voice trails off.

I blink once, twice, three times.

"There's more," she says on an exhale. "Apparently, he hooked up with some girl last night. Beat the shit out of her. Ms. Santini from Three-A was on her way to work and stopped to drop off her trash by the dumpsters. Apparently, she heard a moaning sound. When she saw the girl, her clothes were torn. She was beaten up and started bawling about Carlos..."

My head gets dizzy, but I force myself to hear every detail. "An ambulance took her away, but she was in pretty bad shape."

I want to ask more questions, but the terror has a clamp on my throat.

"I think you need to stay close to me for a while, okay? The Snakes are getting more aggressive. They want the Blue Houses as their own territory, and it looks like they're trying to instill some bigger fear on the streets." She drops her gaze. I know she's afraid. Every girl in the Blue Houses probably heard the story by now.

"Yeah. Okay. I'll make sure Angelo knows I need to leave before it gets dark out."

"Good idea. We need to sync our schedules so you aren't walking alone at night. I'm gonna talk to some other people and try to get their schedules down so that everyone has a buddy or something at night. I'm sure when everyone hears about this, we won't be the only ones who are scared." I nod my head and stand up mechanically, rinsing my mug and walking to my room to digest the new information. After grabbing my stuff, I check my purse to make sure that my gun is still inside. I lock myself in the bathroom and load and unload the gun a few times, reacquainting myself with the weapon. If Carlos comes, I'll be ready for him.

Getting to work, I let Angelo know the details of what's new with Carlos. He's angry and continues to tell me that I shouldn't be so stubborn and I need to let the Borignones get involved. But I refuse. I still don't want any debts to my name. I've made it this far, and I believe I can wait it out a little longer.

Work passes in a blur. I'm convincing a girl to sell her diamond ring while Angelo sells the two violins and a Cartier watch to an elderly couple who want to buy something for their grandchildren.

When the day is done, Angelo insists on calling a car to take me home. I sigh deeply, knowing that the driver will be one of Angelo's associates. But considering the fact that Carlos is out of jail, I'm not going to complain. I nod my head and take his ride in the name of safety.

I get in the huge black Escalade and see a massive man sitting in the driver's seat. Swallowing hard, I remind myself that he's not an enemy, but on my side. He drives me right up to my building and I gingerly walk out, my shaking hand inside my purse, gripping my gun. I'm scared as hell, but it makes me feel a modicum of control. The driver enters the building with me and steps into the elevator as well.

We reach the fourth floor when I tell him he can go. "I can get into my apartment fine now." He nods his head wordlessly and re-calls the elevator to bring him back downstairs.

I get up to my door without incident and let out the breath I was holding while I pry my fingers off my gun. "I'm okay," I say out loud, turning my head and letting my gaze run up and down my hallway. It's empty. I pull out my key and step forward onto my threadbare Welcome mat when I feel like I've kicked something. I look down, confused at what's on the floor. It must be Janelle's sweater that she dropped on her way out. I bend down to pick it up and freeze.

A cat. A dead cat. Its neck is broken with eyes that are bugging out. Blood is smeared all over its gray-and-black fur. Images of dead rats being left by Carlos in people's doorways pile into my head. The moment the stench of blood hits my nose, I turn my head and vomit in the hallway. Carlos. He's back. And he hasn't forgotten about me.

CHAPTER 13

When my stomach is empty, I step over the dead cat and enter my apartment, locking myself in the bathroom. My mind races. "What do I do? What the fuck do I do? I need to call Janelle." With my body shaking, and sweat pouring down my face, I pick up my phone and manage to dial her number. It rings and rings, my heart pounding. *Pick up, Janelle!*

When I get her voicemail, I hang up and dial again. On the fourth try, I realize she isn't going to answer. "Help! I need her. I need help!" My heart is pounding harder now, and I feel like I'll be sick again. I focus my gaze on the bathroom wall, paint cracking along the edge.

I drop onto the floor, dropping my head into my hands. "Carlos. He's back and he's going to kill me. My mom said I should just give into him. Maybe I should end my misery and just call him. At least I won't have to wait for him to find me. No, I can't do that. Could I?"

I force myself up and into my bedroom, opening my side table, and pulling open the drawer. I find the stack of folded papers for prospective colleges underneath Janelle's beauty samples from Sephora. I sit on my bed and ruffle through them. Princeton. Yale. Columbia. I try to take in a few deep breaths, but my nausea intensifies. "I can't give into Carlos. I need to stand strong. Just a few more months. But how?"

Visions of the dead cat flashback in front of my eyes. I run back to the toilet to dry heave. When my body understands there's nothing left inside me to puke, I sit up and lean against the cold tile wall. "I've got a dead animal and a pile of vomit by my front door. I need to clean it up, but I can't. I just can't do it."

Like a flash through my head: "Angelo. I need to call Angelo. He'll know what to do. Does removing the dead body of a cat count as a favor to the Borignones? Maybe it does. But I have no other option right now."

He answers on the third ring. "Hey, doll. Everything okay?" His voice is laced with concern.

"No, Angelo. Something's happened. It's Carlos—"

"Take a breath. I can't hear you and everything sounds muffled."

I inhale and exhale deeply a few times, opening my mouth to speak again. "Carlos. He's b-back. He left a dead cat on my doorstep!" I pant. "It's there." My voice is frantic, chest shaking. "I threw up—" Gasp. "I puked ev-ev-everywhere." I exhale, trying to compose myself so I can speak while fluids fall from every crevice of my face. "I can't go back out. There's b-blood. A cat. He left me a dead cat—"

"Okay," he says calmly while I grip the phone like a lifeline. "I'm out in Jersey right now on business, and won't be back until work in the morning. But don't worry—I'm going to send Stix back to you, all right? He'll be there. Same guy who brought you home. Remember, he's very tall and built. Long black hair and green eyes. He'll knock three times on your door. Do not open the door unless you hear that knock, got it? Three times."

"Y-yeah, Angelo. I got it. I r-r-remember him."

"He'll clean it all up for you. Do you have a friend you can call and stay with tonight? You can't be alone there. Janelle workin' late?"

"Uh-huh. I think she said she was staying at her boyfriend's after work... I—"

"And that good-for-nothing piece of shit mom of yours. Fuckin' Irina." He practically spits out her name. "Probably on some bender." He lets out a breath over the phone.

"You gotta call a friend, okay? No stayin' alone tonight. Get outta that shit hole. If you can't think of anyone, I'll arrange for you to go somewhere. We'll talk about all of this shit when we see each other tomorrow. I'm not letting you get hurt, do you understand me? If I need to send a friend a' mine over to stand guard at your door, I'll do it. Maybe you gotta live with me or with that teacher of yours for a while—"

I listen to him intently, my stomach feeling raw. I grip the phone harder, my knuckles turning white. "I'll think of someone to call for tonight."

"I'm gonna call Stix now. He'll be there soon. Call me and we'll make sure you got somewhere to go." He hangs up the phone and my head spins.

Who the hell can I call? Other than Janelle's friends, I have none of my own. I'm afraid if I tell anyone from the Blue Houses, it'll get around what happened to me. And gossip always makes things worse. I bet that's what Carlos wants. He wants to scare the shit out of me and everyone else. He wants to hear that I freaked-the-fuck-out. I know that piece of shit; he gets off on terrorizing people. Even if I could call a friend from the building, I wouldn't put them in that kind of danger. And, if people knew Carlos was after me, they wouldn't want to come anywhere near me! Even Janelle could be in danger right now. What if he uses her to get to me?

My mind keeps moving through all kinds of scenarios when I hear three consecutive knocks at my door. I jump up and nervously walk to my door.

"Who is it?" I say with a shaking voice.

What if Carlos knocked three times? Three times is a perfectly normal number of knocks. I stand on my tippy-toes and stare through the peephole in the front door. It's the driver, Stix. I was so concerned with getting home earlier I didn't take in all of his features. In this moment, I realize how stupid that was. Through the peephole, I give him a once-over, making sure he isn't some random thug pretending to be Stix.

He speaks. "Eve? It's me, Stix. Angelo sent me," he says through the door in a deep voice. "Why don't you just wait inside and let me take care a' this. I'll remove the, uh, animal, and clean the floor for you. Got all my cleaning supplies with me; it was already in the back of my car. Just relax, a'ight? Angelo told me you're like a daughter to him, you don't gotta be scared of me. I'll be quick."

I let out a small squeak in reply before turning around, leaning my back against the door, and sliding to the floor so I'm sitting against it. I press my head back against the door, listening to him work. The sound of him cleaning is soothing.

I hear him grumbling about something and he barks out, "You there?" I knock against the door, letting him know that I'm near.

"The cat is gone now and I'm cleaning the mat with something that's pretty damn strong. Got any Lysol?"

"Uh huh," I reply.

Seconds seem to pass. Minutes maybe. "I'm waitin'."

I finally stand up and walk to my cleaning closet, grabbing the spray. Holding the can reminds me I have a gun. I run into my room and pull it out of my purse. I instantly feel better. I want to open the door, but my stomach suddenly drops. I can't open the door. Terror starts to build again. I feel wetness pouring out of my eyes. I can't do this.

"I can't open the door," I say, my voice quivering.

"Okay. No worries. I got a daughter myself, okay? I said it, but I'll tell you again. I'm cleanin' shit up. No worries." I hear a scrubbing sound again and try to focus on it.

"You still there?" he asks again.

"Yeah," I reply against the door.

"Call a friend. This shit is all clean now."

And with those parting words, he leaves. I look through the peephole to make sure no one is near and let out a breath and text Angelo.

ME: Stix came and left. It's done.

If I can just find someone to be with me for a few hours, maybe Janelle will finally answer the phone and I can be with her tonight. Maybe I can even crash with her on Leo's couch. I try calling her another few times, but still, no answer. My heart pounds. What if she's gone?

I pick up the phone with my heart in my chest, calling her salon. They tell me that she's in the middle of doing someone's highlights and she won't be done until close to ten-thirty. Relief hits me so hard that I try not to bawl.

Janelle may be safe for now, but I still need to get the hell out of here in the meantime. I scroll through my contacts until I find Vincent's name and open up a message. I need to do this quickly before I think too hard about it and chicken out. The cursor blinks and I have no idea what I should type. There's no way in hell I'm going to tell him what happened to me. If he knew, he'd just think of me as some pathetic loser living in a crack den. I want him to see me as more than that. At the same time, I can't stay here alone right now. My lock is bullshit and can probably be cracked open within seconds. Vincent is strong and can protect me...and just the thought of him, of being with him, makes me feel secure. But, I haven't spoken to him in over a month! What if he doesn't want to hear from me? I look up again at the stack of college stuff spread out on my bed, and it gives me the strength I need. I'm doing this. Deep in my gut, I know that being with him right now is the right move. I need to at least try.

CHAPTER 14

My fingers move at lightning speed as I type Vincent a text; I need to move quickly before I change my mind.

ME: Hey. What's up? It's Eve

What if he doesn't reply? Shit. Maybe I made a mistake?

VINCENT: Eve. Hey.

Oh my God! He replied. My hands shake as I type out the next message

ME: Want to hang out tonight?

VINCENT: Yeah, was just about to workout. Wanna join?

ME: Sure

VINCENT: I'll be there in 30

ME: OK

I lock myself in the bathroom and sit against the white tile wall, clutching my gun with one hand and my cell phone with the other. Thirty minutes, that's all I need to wait. Vincent will come, and I'll be okay. I know that I'll be safe with him. I have to be.

I shut my eyes, trying to focus my attention on the man I'm about to see. Vincent's huge callused hands. Vincent's strong body. Vincent's deep and dark eyes. Vincent's brilliant mind.

I finally stand myself up and head to the sink, washing my face methodically. I need to calm myself down if I'm going to see him. Stepping out of the bathroom, I move to my bedroom and change out of my jeans and into some loose sweats; I barely notice what I'm putting on other than the fact that it's comfortable.

I glance at the clock. It's been twenty-five minutes since we texted. Is he almost here? I risk a peek out my bedroom window when I see some thugs from the Snakes hanging out on the steps by the front door, their red and black bandanas clear under the lamplights by the stoop.

"Shit!" I exclaim. The last thing I need is for Vincent to have a run-in with Carlos' crew on his way to me.

Another dose of dread runs through my veins as I watch Vincent's black Range Rover park in front of the building. He walks out of his car, his steps sure and gait long. I can only imagine the don't-fuck-with-me face he's probably sporting. I briefly wonder again who this man is, completely unafraid? Vincent steps up to enter the building when the Snakes stand to greet him. I swallow back the bile rising in my throat. Should I run downstairs and warn him? Yell out the window?

I want to open my mouth to scream, "No," but all that will come out is a low and painful rasp.

Vincent takes the hat off his head. The Cartel stands up. A moment later, I watch as they run off the stoop. "What?"

He walks up the two small steps, looking left and right, entering the building confidently. I walk to the kitchen, grab a cup and turn on the faucet. I fill it to the top and drink it all down. I'm under so much stress right now that I can barely think straight. I probably saw wrong. I must have. Maybe they got a phone call and ran off, having nothing to do with Vincent.

I hear a knock at my door. What if it it's Carlos? My feet are frozen to the floor. I hear another pounding noise, like brick against wood. I force myself to step to the door, my body quaking as I stand on my tiptoes to look through the peephole. A whoosh of relief covers me when I see that it is, in fact, Vincent.

"Just a second," I manage to stutter out.

I look inside my bag, making sure my gun is still where I left it last. Breathing deeply, I remind myself to act upbeat. Nothing happened. Everything is just fine.

I swing the door open and step out before he can get a look inside my apartment. But as my feet touch the Welcome mat, I jump off as if I've been burned while my stomach sinks with echoes of memory.

He watches my skittish behavior with concern. "Eve?" His brows are furrowed as he bends down, getting a closer look at my face, seemingly trying to see what's got me acting so strangely. My eyes must look red-rimmed and inflamed considering how much crying I recently did.

"Hey Vincent!" My voice is so phony I barely believe it myself. "Ready for the gym? Wild night you've got planned. Hope you don't mind me crashing." I'm talking too quickly and let out an awkward laugh.

He holds my hand possessively, eyes roaming up and down the decrepit hallway.

"You've been crying." It's a statement, not a question.

I blink, but he doesn't say more.

As we get off the elevator, I start second guessing all of my choices. Maybe I shouldn't have left my apartment? What if Carlos is downstairs? Before Vincent notices my stress, he opens the front door. I let out a whimper of relief; the stoop is completely empty.

He opens his car door and helps me step inside before slamming it shut. Jogging around to the driver's seat, he gets inside, buckles up, and starts the engine.

I'm still reeling as his thumb begins to graze across my knuckles. His touch is so soothing. Ninety-nine percent of myself wants to curl into a ball in his arms and just tell him everything. But that tiny little one percent has some pride. I simply refuse to look any more pathetic to him than I already do.

I stare at his strong profile, wondering how many women he's been with. He's probably slept with more girls than I can count on both of my hands a few times over. And here I am, a naïve virgin from the hood.

He stops the car at a red light and turns to me. "Eve? I can see the stress in your face." I immediately clam up with his observation. The light turns green and I watch as his eyes dart between me and the road, waiting for me to reply.

"It's nothing. Just a stupid fight with my sister," I lie, my eyes glancing out my window.

"You're lying," he tells me simply.

He parks in a small outdoor parking lot and steps out of the car, and I let myself out before he can walk around to open my door. We cross the quiet street to a large warehouse. Vincent rings up to Floor Two, the buzzer sounds and the lock opens. He holds the door for me as I walk inside. The staircase is narrow, with just enough room for us to walk in single file. Vincent starts up first, and I quietly trail behind him.

We get up to Joe's Gym—which is a lot larger than it seems from outside—a standard boxing ring is in the center of the room, surrounded by clusters of red and blue mats, jump ropes, boxing gloves, and other gym equipment. Vincent walks us to the far corner and tells me to hang out while he uses the locker room. I don't need to change, but I pull off my sweatshirt and use it to cover my purse, leaving it all in the corner. I drop myself on a large blue mat and look down at my outfit.

"Oh shit," I say out loud, grimacing. I'm in a pair of ratty old gray sweatpants and a T-shirt Leo gave to Janelle last year. It's long and baggy, hanging down to my knees. At least it's black.

Vincent steps out of the locker room and jogs over to a muscular guy in the middle of the ring. They talk and keep looking over at me while I self-consciously bring my knees to my chest. Is he going to tell me to go home? I can't go home yet. I turn around and dig into my purse, checking to see if Janelle called me. She still hasn't. I just need Vincent to stay with me until Janelle is off from work.

"Ten-thirty," I repeat to myself.

He jogs back to me. "All right. I'm not gonna fight tonight. Instead, I'm gonna teach you some shit."

"Um, me?" I squeak, looking up at him nervously.

He chuckles, throwing a heavy arm around my small shoulders. "Yeah, you. I'll teach you some kicks and punches. How to get out of some holds. Maybe even a little grappling."

I step back to protest, but he immediately crosses his arms in front of his chest in a stance that's telling me he isn't taking *no* for an answer. I sigh.

"Whenever shit gets tough in life, it's good to exert some physical energy. I'm not going to push you into talking, but we both know that something went down tonight. You'd be surprised, but working out has a way of clearing shit up mentally." I want to argue, but he shuffles me forward to the center of the mat before I can get a word in.

He turns me to face him. "Don't ever lie to me, Eve. I'll always know it. Understand?" I swallow the saliva in my mouth. I'm staring at the Bull right now, who clearly does what he wants when he wants.

I've still got at least two more hours to waste before Janelle can call me. If I want to stay with him right now, I have no choice but to go along with his plan.

I shake out my shoulders, trying to focus. "All right. Let's do this," I tell him. He smiles, trying not to laugh at my attempt to warm up.

"Let's start on the bag." We walk to a large red punching bag hanging from the ceiling. He demonstrates basic kicks and punches. I do my best to mimic his stance and the way he turns his arms with each punch and kick. Shifting my body this way and that, he's seemingly obsessed with proper form. When I've got the hang of the basics, Vincent shouts out my first combination.

Again and again, I front kick, jab left, and jab right. "There we go, Eve. Very good." He nods. "Let's do that another seven times." He counts off, pacing around me as sweat beads on my forehead.

"Stop," he commands, his voice deep. In some strange way, it feels good to just trust him and take orders. I'm not in any state of mind to make choices right now, even small ones. He may be dominating, but he isn't cruel.

Vincent steps back to the bag, holding it steady with both hands. "I want to see round-house left, round-house right, jab, jab, punch, and elbow." He demonstrates and I stare with heavy breaths and rapt attention. The strength and power of his body is obvious in every move he makes; he's so thick and muscular, but at the same time, has so much speed and agility. It's clear why he's such a monster in the ring. I copy his moves again and again, hitting the bag with all of my might, while he circles me, yelling, "Harder, Eve. Three More! Punch harder!" All I can hear are his shouts, and it's keeping my mind focused on nothing other than the task at hand.

He tells me to stop, and I drop my hands to my knees. My entire body is no longer simply damp, but wet with perspiration. Ignoring my exhaustion, he shows me how to swing my arms laterally from wide angles, so that a punch to the temple can be easily followed with an elbow straight to the chin. I stand tall and lift the bottom of my shirt, pressing it against my sweaty forehead. Vincent's eyes roam my body and stop at my face. My breath catches as his pupils dilate. I can't help but stare back, my breathing still labored. His T-shirt is tight against his chest while dark jersey shorts hang low on his narrow hips. He still has his hat on, and it showcases his straight Roman nose and chiseled jaw. He looks intimidating and sexy as hell.

He steps forward, pressing his lips together in a thin line. "I want to show you how to get out of a hold." His voice comes out hoarse. "Let's assume that someone is coming at you from behind and holds your arms against the side of your body." He moves behind me, acting out his words. I feel him harden. I clench my fists, glad that he can't seem my face as I swallow hard.

"You're going to want to drop your weight down as if you're doing a squat. Especially if he's much bigger than you. There's more to the move, but let's begin with that." He slowly releases me.

Vincent steps behind me again and again, restraining me. I do as he asks and drop down in a squat. "Keep your feet wider than hip width," he commands. My thighs burn, but I refuse to give up.

I'm about to squat down again, but this time, he doesn't allow me to drop. Instead, he holds me firmly in place. While I'm not in any pain, it's clear he isn't about to let me move without his consent. The rational side of my mind lets me know that he's probably about to show me the rest of the move. But another part of my mind begins to panic.

I struggle against him, but his huge, masculine body is unshakeable. I can feel his dick against my back, and my entire body starts to buzz, terror filling every crevice of my body.

I hear my name being called, but it's nothing but a distant sound on a stranger's lips. I feel someone turning me around, but I can't look up. I hear a voice, but it's muffled as the whooshing sound in my ears increases in volume.

I see Vincent gripping my shoulders and staring into my face. But my vision feels fuzzy as the panic pulls me under. Am I drowning?

I think I hear my name, but it's far away. Little by little, it gets louder and louder until finally, it's clear.

"Eve," Vincent calls. "It's me. Breathe, baby." His voice full of worry and anguish as his hands move up and down my back. "Calm down. It's just me. I'm here." He gently places me in a chair and drops to his knees in front of me. Somehow the tension in my body settles, turning into numbness.

"Vincent?" I croak. He wipes the tears off my face with his thumbs. "It's over now, okay?" He holds me tightly and I can feel exhaustion settling into my bones.

"Over? No," I say, staring up at the clock. Janelle isn't done with work yet. I can't go home. "It's not done. I'm not ready to give up. I want more, Vincent—"

"Baby, we've been going at it for over an hour. This isn't giving up—"

"I want to do more! I can handle it," I beg. He shakes his head, not understanding what's happening. "Don't take me home, Vincent. Please. I'm not ready to go home," I sob, pleading with him.

He seems to understand that going home is not an option. "Let's go back to my apartment. You aren't going back there," he tells me firmly. My breath hitches and I nod my head in utter relief.

"I should call my s-sister," I stutter.

"No problem. Call her. Tell her you're out tonight."

Before I can put on my sweatshirt, Vincent grabs his and slides it over my head, pulling my damp ponytail out of the hood.

"I have my shirt," I gasp. The tears won't stop running down my face.

"I know. But mine is warmer." Without thinking, I lift the bottom of his sweatshirt and put it to my nose, inhaling deeply. It smells just like him, and the scent soothes me.

I take my phone out of my bag and with shaking hands, text Janelle.

ME: I'm staying out tonight. Stay at Leo's. DO NOT GO HOME.

JANELLE: What's going on?? It's Carlos, right? Who are you with?? I'm waiting for client's color to set. I need another forty min before I can call...

ME: Ms. Levine. Don't worry.

I type out the lie and immediately bite my lip. I can't get into the details of Vincent right now, especially not over text. I'll explain it all to her later. She'll understand.

JANELLE: OK.

I put my phone away as Vincent lifts me up off the mat and into his arms. "Vincent, I can w-walk," I tell him, my voice still staccato from crying.

"No. I want to take care of you right now. Let me." I lean my forehead into his neck and relax into his arms.

I shut my eyes while he drives and slowly doze off. "Eve, we're here," he whispers, putting his hands on the side of my face. I open my eyes with a start and look around. We're in a parking lot on the corner of Houston and Wooster Street. Vincent opens the door for me and we walk together into a beautiful white building. The doorman nods to us as Vincent shuffles me to the elevator. At the penthouse floor, we step off. He pulls out his keys, unlocking three different locks. After typing in a complicated-looking code to an alarm panel, he opens the door. The minute my eyes take in what's around me, I gasp. The entire kitchen, living room, and dining room is an open floor plan. The kitchen gleams in marble and chrome, a beautiful white marble island separating it from the dining area. A long wooden table surrounded by black chairs serves as the dining room. Farthest away is a living area, complete with a beautiful L-shaped black leather couch, coffee table, and big screen TV.

He clears his throat and I snap my jaw shut. "Let me show you to the bathroom. You wash up and I'll order us some Chinese. Cool?" I nod my head in silence as he takes my hand. Opening a door at the end of the living area, we walk through a short corridor. "Here's my bedroom," he points. The room is cozy in whites, grays, and blacks. A large bed sits in the center of the room with two wooden side tables flanking it. A wooden desk is in the corner, piled high with books and a silver laptop. The space is clean, orderly, and masculine. It's exactly what I'd imagine Vincent's room to look like.

"I've got some clean clothes in the drawer by the bedside table. Take whatever you need. The bathroom is right there." He points to another door and I nod my head. "Let me just get you some fresh towels." He steps into the hallway and returns a moment later with a large fluffy white towel and a smaller one. He hands them to me and then steps out.

"Holy shit," I say in a whisper as the door closes. Walking to the window, Vincent has the perfect view of West Houston Street. I can see the Angelika Theatre straight ahead. Stepping into his bathroom, my eyes widen; it's completely white marble. Turning on the shower and taking off my clothes, I step into the spray. I sigh in relief at the heavy water pressure. I grab his shampoo, washing my hair and focusing on the clean scent. I use a simple bar of Dove soap, and I shut my eyes, imagining Vincent using this same bar to clean his own body. I swallow, set down the soap, and lean against the shower wall. I wish I could stay in this apartment forever.

Shutting off the shower and stepping out, I wrap myself up with the towel. Moving back into his bedroom, I pull out a plain white T-shirt and a pair of sweatpants from his drawer. I have to roll them up on my hips seven or eight times to keep from falling off me. I brush out my hair with a comb that I find underneath his sink and tie it back in a braid using my hair tie. I'm going to eat with him, ask to see a movie, and feign sleep on his couch. I realize I'm being a liar right now, but my life is at stake here.

I finally garner the strength to leave the room. My bare feet pitter-patter against the wooden floor as I enter his living area. Vincent leans against the marble kitchen island, staring at his cell phone. He lifts his head, noticing my entrance. The moment our eyes lock, I swear to God, my heart stops. He looks me over from my toes up to my face, his eyes darkening. I immediately feel nervous. Should I not have used his clothes?

"Food is on its way up." His voice is deep and low.

I take a seat at the dining table, curling my feet beneath my butt. The doorbell rings and Vincent moves to get it, handing cash to the delivery guy and telling him to keep the change. Moving back to the table, he sets everything up. I dig in, eating like I haven't had a decent meal in days. It dawns on me that I skipped lunch at work, assuming I'd eat a big dinner at home. But obviously, those plans didn't work out.

"Where have you been?" I ask quietly, chewing a piece of steamed broccoli covered in garlic sauce.

"Busy." I wait for him to elaborate, but he doesn't. "You ready to tell me what that was about before?"

I drop my head as my heart beats heavily. "No...I...I can't." I shake my head.

"Eve," he places his fork in front of him, turning to me with warm eyes. "You can and you will. Do you trust me?" His hands move to my thighs, but it isn't sexual. It's comforting.

I slowly nod my head as he moves closer to me, taking my hand in his. "Talk to me. Let me help you." My guard lowers from his gentle words.

I open my mouth, and like an open faucet, the words burst out in a rush. I give him the backstory on the Snakes. Surprisingly, he barely shows alarm. I tell him how the Cartel somehow managed to come at the right time, saving me from a potential gang rape. When I get to the dead cat, I'm shaking so badly that he has no choice but to hold me tight to keep me from crumbling.

"Holy shit, Eve." He gently caresses my back. "Okay. I'm here now. You don't have to worry." His voice sounds strong and confident. He continues to secure me to his body as I cry harder, unsure how many more tears I have left to shed. My body feels exhausted and rung-out.

"You deserve more than this. So much more. I've done enough selfish shit in my twenty-one years on this earth. And for all the messed-up things I've done, I'm going to do right by you. I'm going to take care of this. Do you hear me?" I shudder in his arms, wanting so badly to believe him. "Let me get you a glass of water." He moves to stand, but I grab onto him, refusing to let go. He sets his body back down.

"Vincent, who a-are you?" I ask, searching his face for answers.

"I don't want to give you details. Let's just say, you don't have space in your life right now for a man like me." He slowly exhales. "But you already know who I am in here, don't you?" He presses my hand to his heart.

I raise my eyebrows, vaguely remember our conversation by my front door. "Does it have to do with duality, Batman?" I let out a shaky smile.

He rubs the side of my face with his palm. "Yeah, baby. Exactly that." He pushes his hair back, resigned. "What we have between us right now may not be total openness, but I won't ever lie to you, either. If I can't answer something, I'd rather stay quiet than give you a bullshit story. You deserve better than that."

"But, how will you take care of this for me? These men—Vincent, you don't understand—they're dangerous!" My voice comes out as a plea.

He smoothes the lines on my forehead with his thumbs while he lets out an ironic laugh. "My life is seriously fucked up, Eve. Let's just say, my father runs a major business. My family and I, we're very well-connected people. You can trust I'll get this taken care of." He locks his eyes with mine and I tilt my head to the side, still not completely comprehending; I wish that he would give it to me straight.

"Are you going into business with him after college?"

"I already work for him. Have since I turned eighteen. And until I met you, I never let myself imagine another path was possible. I've got some ideas going through my head now, which I'm trying to make work. But until then, all we can be is friends. That's what I've got to offer." I blink a few times, trying to hold back my tears. "But even if you don't want my friendship, understand that Carlos is finished."

I slowly nod my head, my breathing settling down. I want to argue with him! I can handle whatever it is he's hiding. I want more than just friendship. Hell, I want it all. But a nagging part of my brain tells me that he's right; I can't add more to my plate right now. "I'm just so tired, Vincent," my voice is low.

He stands, taking my hand in his and walking us into his bedroom. I climb into his huge bed as he turns out lights and flips on a small lamp, casting shadows around us.

"I want to be able to see you," he says softly, sitting beside me. I sit up on my knees, staring at his features.

He opens the drawer in his nightstand and takes out a bottle of lotion. Squeezing some into his palm, he starts to methodically massage my hands with the cream. I let out a hum, feeling soothed by his touch.

"The hands hold a lot of tension." His voice is gruff. "This should re-lax you." I open my eyes. The heated look on his face sends a zing straight through my core.

"Vincent?" I say his name reverently, wanting to repeat it over and over again. His name on my lips feels undeniably right. "Do you...like me?" My voice is so quiet, I can barely hear myself.

He sets his hands down, moving them to my sides. "Eve." He lets out a troubled sigh. "I like you more than I've ever liked anything. I've never given a shit about any woman before you. There have been so many girls—" he winces, realizing his mistake as my heart plunges down. "But they've all been faceless and nameless. Since I met you, there has been no one else. You're all I can see."

"But, why do you keep disappearing on me? Why can't we—"

"Listen closely, okay? My life, as it currently stands, is not meant for you. One day, maybe. But not yet. You have your own journey right now. You've got to get your ass out of the Blue Houses. Get into college, right? Nothing else matters other than that."

I move back as if I've been slapped. "Not...meant for me?" I repeat, my voice stuttering. Does he mean I'm not good enough for him?

He takes my hands back in his. "It's not what you think. But right now, this friendship we've got is all there can be. I won't get you wrapped up in my life. Promise me that you will focus on nothing other than your studies." He touches the side of my face and I screw my eyes shut, unable to stop myself from leaning into his warm palm.

He clears his throat. "Repeat after me." I gaze up at him, unable to look away. "Vincent thinks I'm gorgeous."

I stay quiet. "Come on, Eve, I want to hear it."

"Vincent thinks I'm gorgeous," I hesitantly repeat.

He smirks, continuing. "Vincent thinks I'm brilliant." I can feel my face turn pink. "I'm waiting, Eve. Tick-tock…"

"Vincent thinks I'm brilliant." I shut my eyes again and smile wide, too shy to look at the man giving me this praise.

"Vincent thinks that I'm going to leave the life I'm living behind me, and be whoever I want to be. He won't let his shit fall on me." His voice is full of promise.

I open my eyes and stare at him openly, wishing that everything he says will be true someday. "I want to be a lawyer," I tell him reluctantly, unsure of what his response will be.

"Oh yeah? I can see that." He quirks his lips to the side.

I can feel a glimmer of hope turning in my chest. "Really?"

He moves his head without doubt. "Yes. I can help you with that too when the time comes. Go to sleep now. You're safe here with me." I settle down with my head on his pillow as he lightly strokes my hair.

"Vincent?" I ask quietly.

"Yeah, baby." His hands move to massage up and down my back.

"What do we have between us? We have something special, right?" I turn around to face him. We may not be able to be together, but I know in my heart that we have something more than just friendship. This can't be one-sided; I know deep down he feels it, too.

He pauses, seemingly thinking of the right response. "Yeah, we've got something. But what we have has nothing to do with anyone else on earth. What we have between us, is just for us."

He moves me on top of him and lets his hands rub from my toes all the way up into my hair. Even though he's obviously holding a hell of a lot back from me, something inside me is pushing me to just enjoy this moment and trust him. His touch feels so good. So right.

"Can I kiss you?" I suck in a breath, wanting him so badly but also, so afraid.

His hand slides over my hip, slowly dragging the sweatpants from my legs. "I love how delicate you are. Soft. You're a siren on a quiet street. You're all I hear." His words tune and bind me to him.

I feel his warm mouth against the side of my lips and a tiny moan escapes. I want him to be on top of me but he grips my thighs, not letting me move. "You're in control tonight, understand?"

He sits up with me straddling him and I immediately turn my head to the side, too nervous to look into his eyes. "Don't turn away from me," he orders. I slowly turn back, nervous that it'll be the hard version of Vincent in front of me. Instead, there's nothing but warmth shining from his face. "It's me here, just me. I'll never hurt you."

I feel his lips on my neck and gasp as he trails his warm mouth up, pausing beneath my ear. Moving to my lips, he kisses me chastely, over and over again.

I want more, my body hums. I grind my hips down onto his pelvis. I can tell he's keeping himself steady, letting me set the pace. His warm tongue dips into my mouth and my body melts deeper into his lap. His parts press against mine, and I yearn to feel more of his weight on me. I tug on his arm and move off his lap, laying down on the mattress. With my eyes, I'm urging him to follow. He's hesitant, as if he really needs to make sure that I'm okay and feeling stable. He checks me over and I give him a small nod of approval. My throat is dry, but I have never felt safer in my entire life.

His hands move into my hair, pulling out the tie. My damp strands fall around us as he pushes himself into me, wrapping his arms around my back and pressing me harder against his solidness. We're kissing mindlessly when his knee snakes up between my legs. It's as if an alarm goes off in my mind and I immediately want to tear off his clothes. *Oh, God.*

I tug on the bottom of his shirt desperately. He sits up, pulling it up and over his head.

"Ohhh," my voice says of its own accord; nothing we've ever done comes close to *this.* His body looks as if it's been chiseled from granite. He sits me up, taking off my shirt. I melt as his eyes take their fill, clearly liking what he sees.

He lowers his head, letting his tongue lave at my nipple. I liquefy, grabbing his hair with my hands and moaning as he nips and tugs at my breast. Moving to the next side, he kisses and sucks until I'm writhing against him in pleasure.

He moves himself, pulling up one of my thighs and wrapping it against his waist. Pressing himself into me as if we're having sex, I can't stop moaning. His pants are still on and so is my underwear, but I swear on my life I never knew that something could feel this good.

"Everything about you, Eve," he rasps. "I want to strip you naked." He presses again, deeper. "I want to lick you until you're screaming my name."

My body is shaking so hard right now that I think I may pass out. "Vincent, Vincent, Vincent," is all I can manage. "I'm so—" my voice is hoarse as he grips my thigh harder, lifting it up over his shoulder.

"Look at me." His voice is hard and demanding. I open my eyes, locking my gaze to his. He leans his head down, breathing in my breaths. Open mouths. Tongues. I'm sweaty and wet all over. He slides his hands up, brushing his callused fingers over my nipples again and again. I'm squeezing my core in pulses, my body finding a rhythm. All at once, my legs straighten out and my toes curl as I come apart beneath him.

He stops, holding me tight as he whispers in my ear. "You're perfect. Do you know how wonderful you are?" I wrap my arms around his back, my throat raspy from how loud I must have been. "You're shaking." He turns me so that I'm back on top of him, holding me tight while our breathing settles.

"D-do you need—" I feel how hard he is, and realize that he probably needs something in return.

"You don't need to do this tonight, Eve," he whispers in my ear. "This isn't about me."

"I want to." I push forward, eager to feel him.

"Are you sure?" he continues, lowering his mouth to my nipple, taking a slow and lazy lick. "My tongue sucking on your nipples while you touch me? Or maybe, you want to feel my stubble rubbing between your thighs while I take my time?" My body short-circuits from his words as I stroke him over his pants.

"I want to drink you in. Just the thought of licking you…" I gasp as he sucks hard at my nipples. "You feel how hard I am?" We're both dripping with sweat as I finally put my hand into his underwear, feeling his hardness jump directly into my palm. I felt how big he was through his clothes, but this is entirely different. He's huge, hot, and velvet soft.

I'm tentative, unsure what I should do. He moves his hand over mine, covering my fingers with his, showing me how he likes it.

I continue at the pace he sets when he finally lets go of my hand and brings me closer to him. He slides his tongue around my nipple again, bringing it back into his mouth. I let myself grip his dick harder and we both moan until we're panting again from pleasure. "Don't let go, baby. I'm so close."

He screws his eyes shut and comes with a guttural shout. I feel him coat my hand and my eyes widen. I don't dare to move as his body tremors. I'm in awe; watching Vincent come is amazing.

"Holy fuck, Eve…" His wide chest glistens with sweat, and I lick my lips.

"I should wash—"

He nods, sprawling himself out on the bed while I stand up and walk to the bathroom. Looking at myself in his mirror, I take in a breath at what I see. My face is flushed pink, hair wild. My lips are puffy and my nipples are all red. I'm in a state of utter amazement right now; intimacy with Vincent is bliss.

Vincent steps into the bathroom, moving directly behind me. We're both staring at each other in the mirror, smiling and satisfied. The top of my head hits the center of his chest, and for the first time in forever, I decide that I love feeling so small. Even with all our physical differences, or maybe because of them, we look perfect together.

I turn on the warm water and place my hands in the sink when he slides his hands on top of mine. Taking the soap, he cleans each of my fingers one by one. I lean back into his chest, savoring the feeling of his touch while he cleans me off.

We move back into the bed together and I giggle as he jumps on top of me, putting his nose into my neck and scenting me. He holds my hands together above my head while he puts his face between my breasts, nuzzling me. I'm wheezing with laughter as Vincent's playful side comes out.

"You're embarrassing me, Vincent! Stop! I probably stink!"

He finally moves himself back up, face turning serious. "No, baby." He rubs his nose against my neck. "You literally smell like heaven on earth. Don't you know?" I wrap my legs around his waist, locking him against me.

Part of me wishes we were naked. But another part knows the beauty of this moment is amplified because of the innocence. We both know that he could have taken everything from me, but he didn't.

I burrow my head in his chest, so thankful for him.

"I'm gonna shower now. Give me a few." He kisses me on the temple and stands up. I turn to my side, getting an eyeful of his perfect butt.

After he shuts the door, I check the bedside clock; it's just after midnight. I wait patiently for him to finish. Climbing back into the bed, I burrow into his hard and clean chest and finally, doze off to sleep.

CHAPTER 15

The next morning when I wake up, I find myself alone in Vincent's huge bed. Finding a spare toothbrush in the cabinet in his guest bathroom, I wash myself up as best I can without my usual toiletries. My eyes are still red-rimmed and puffy from all my crying, but deep in my soul, I know that somehow, Vincent will take care of Carlos for me.

Vincent, Vincent, Vincent. I want to say his name a million times, but every time I even think of his name, I flush. The man has somehow taken over everything. I was with him all night and now I feel as if I'm going through a withdrawal. My body aches for more of him. Where is he?

Walking into his beautiful kitchen, I see a note on the dining table. He went out for a run and will be back at nine. Looking up at the clock hanging on his wall, I see that it's already eight forty-five in the morning. I open his fancy refrigerator—surprised to see it's completely stocked. Taking out eggs, milk, and bacon, I hope that when he gets back he's hungry. Opening one of the refrigerator doors, I find it full of fresh vegetables.

The front door opens and shuts, and I turn toward it, nerves fluttering in my stomach. Vincent's hair is damp with sweat and his white T-shirt sticks to his muscular chest. Dark stubble is already growing on his face, even though he was freshly shaven last night. He's so insanely hot that my heart skips at the sight of him. But when we make eye contact, I realize that something's missing. It's Vincent, but his eyes look…uncaring. I feel whiplash from the coolness of his stare. Did he change his mind?

"Morning," he says curtly, and my heart sinks.

He struts into his bedroom without another word, and I hear the shower turn on. I hurry up and scramble fresh eggs with some milk, turning the heat on another pan to fry up the thick-cut bacon. Quickly looking at a recipe from the Food Network on my phone, I put together a small tomato and cucumber salad. God, to have this much food in your fridge at any given time!

Ten minutes later, he's back out in the kitchen freshly showered, and I'm pulling out the whole-wheat toast from the toaster oven. He comes up behind me and I shut my eyes tightly for a moment, savoring his fresh scent.

"You cook?" His voice is full of surprise as he watches me plate the food.

"Yeah. I cook a lot actually…" I want to say more, but the vibe he's giving off is completely closed. Did I say something to anger him? "I hope you don't mind—"

"I don't," he abruptly replies. "And thank you." He nods as I hand him his plate. He stands, waiting by the table until I wash off my hands and come next to him. He doesn't sit until after I do.

We eat together in silence, but the quiet has turned to painful. In the light of day, it's like he's completely shut down from me. I want to yell, ask what the hell happened? I spend my entire breakfast playing our night over, wondering what I said to make this all go so wrong.

"The food is amazing." I turn to him, my heart fluttering from his compliment. I never would have imagined that feeding him would feel this satisfying, but it does.

"You're welcome," I tell him quietly, searching his eyes for a sign he still cares.

Soon afterward, he drives me back to my apartment. The car ride is completely quiet, I can hear horns beeping and fire trucks screaming in the distance. I remember that it's Sunday, and I need to open Angelo's in two hours. On one hand, I'm dreading work, but on the other, I could use something to keep me occupied while my mind runs circles.

He brings me up to my door, and I feel my heart rate pick up. There are a million things I want to ask him.

"Let me come in, check out the place before you go inside."

"No!" I exclaim, putting my hands up. He looks at me skeptically, but the truth is that the last thing I want is for him to see my shit-box apartment. Especially after I just saw his place—I can't imagine what he'd think if he saw mine.

"I'm sure my mom or sister is home. You don't need to go in."

He looks like he wants to argue with me, but thankfully, he doesn't. "I'm going to wait here. You go inside, and when you think everything is okay, come out to tell me. And if something is wrong, yell and I'll run right in." I nod my head, swallowing back my tears. I need to get inside before I lose it in front of him.

His eyes are full of anguish as he steps closer to me, letting his fingers run across my face. "Everything I told you last night—it's still on. No more fear, okay? Trust me. Carlos will never bother you again."

I nod my head, feeling true relief. At the same time though, it seems like he's saying goodbye in a final sense.

"We're still f-friends, right?"

He sighs. "I'll always be your friend, Eve."

The man is holding so much back, and I wish he wouldn't. Before the tears fall, I turn around and open my door, moving inside before he can get a look. Scanning the room, I notice that nothing is out of the ordinary. I step back to the front door, checking through the peephole. He's still there.

I want to tell him all is well, but my tears start falling. I refuse to let him see me cry again. Instead, I pull out my phone and shoot him a quick text. I hear his phone ping and look again through the peephole, watching as he reads it. He curses loudly, slamming his hand down on my door in what looks like anger and frustration. He turns around and stalks away from the door. When I can no longer see him, I feel the emptiness creep back into my chest, as if he took a piece of me with him. I want to throw the door open, chase him down and beg him to take me with him. But instead, my fear cripples me, and I spend the next twenty minutes crying over him in the shower.

Once I calm myself down, I go to work where I talk to Angelo. Again, I refuse any help from the Borignones. I tell him that I slept at a friend's last night who has pretty deep connections. I've got a guarantee that Carlos won't bother me anymore. He looks at me incredulously, but I stand firm. I've still got hope that Vincent will fix this.

When work is over, Angelo insists that he wants to bring me home so he can check out my apartment before I go inside. He's thinking about installing some cameras at my front door for extra surveillance, and I agree it might be a good idea.

Getting back to the Blue Houses, he struts inside the building, glaring at anyone who dares to look at him. We enter my apartment and he searches every possible crevice. When he finally decides that all is safe, he heads out, hugging me to his chest. "You sleep with your phone next to you, okay? And the gun under your pillow. I wish you'd stay with me tonight—"

"I know. But Janelle will be home. And I'll be okay," I tell him nervously.

"You don't always gotta be so tough, Eve. I'm here." He looks at me with pain in his eyes.

"I know you are. Look…I'm going to call you before I sleep, okay? And when I wake up."

"You better." He brings me back for a tight embrace and I realize that in all the ways that matter, Angelo is my father. "Bye, sweetheart." He walks out, shutting the door behind him. I'm closing the front door lock and move to the refrigerator to take out something to eat when I see a note innocuously taped to the door. I pause, confused at first. But when I see the sloppy handwriting, dread pools low in my stomach.

Eve,

I know you've been talking to the cops bout me, and I'm gonna pay U back for that shit. You think I don't see how you think you're better than everyone round here? People like you run to the cops. You're a snitch. A bitch. But before I end you, I'm going to fuck the hell outta you. It's time to pay up.

You see, the truth is that I've been watching you for years. With your baggy clothes and bag full of books. You think that no one noticed you hiding behind your sister? With a face like a fucking angel and a body made for fucking… hiding ain't possible. And now that I've seen what you got underneath all those clothes…you bet I'm gonna tap that. I'm gonna tap it nice and hard until you're begging for fucking mercy.

That cat is just the start, bitch.

I sit at my kitchen table in a trance. He was in here. With the locks being so shitty, I don't know why I should be surprised. Carlos is a sick thug who loves the terror; he loves the game. I have to think of something. I've got to get myself out of this. Vincent said he'd fix it, but maybe Angelo is right. Maybe I need to get the Borignones involved. Obviously, calling the police is completely out of the question. I swallow hard, mind pinging back and forth.

He isn't going to stop until someone puts an end to him. That much is clear. How long will it even take for Vincent to fix this? And that's IF he can fix it. I don't think Vincent understands who Carlos is and who he's dealing with. The Borignones are looking more and more like my only option.

Before I make any rash decisions, I should make a list. I've got too much shit piling up in my head and it's adding to my stress. I take out a pen and piece of paper from the cabinet drawer.

1. TEXT MS. LEVINE TO ASK ABOUT APPLICATION STATUS
2. TEXT JANELLE TO TOUCH BASE AND MAKE SURE SHE'LL BE HOME TONIGHT
3. CRAWL INTO MY BED AND SHUT MY BRAIN OFF
4. WAKE UP AND MAKE ANOTHER LIST DETAILING PROS AND CONS TO LETTING ANGELO TAKE CARE OF CARLOS

I drop my pen and walk into the kitchen, gripping the papers like a lifeline. It's all too much! I need the universe to give me some time—a break to sort out my issues. I can't handle the way my cards are unfolding. While undressing, I take a deep breath, telling myself I can complete things one at a time.

I pull out my phone to text Ms. Levine.

ME: Hey. Any word yet on schools?

MS. L: Soon, Eve. I think in the next week or so, you'll have your answer. Hang in okay?

ME: Yeah. Is there a way you can call admissions? Maybe they can rush their answer or something?

MS. L: I'll call. Don't worry.

I exhale and cross out number one on my list. It's weird, but it feels good to cross off an item. Now it's time to reach Janelle. We texted a few times last night, and I told her we really need to catch up on lots of shit going on.

I haven't been able to tell her about the cat or Vincent and now the letter... I need to talk to her.

ME: Hey Janelle. A lot of shit going on—we need to talk

JANELLE: Is everything all right??? I'm actually at Leo's now. We're going out tonight. I'll be home super late, don't wait up. But I promise I'll be there in the morning.

ME: Ok. Tomorrow morning breakfast before I go to school?

JANELLE: Yup! Love ya. Lock the door! And Juan is home tonight. Call him if you don't want to be alone.

ME: OK. Thanks. BTW, where has Mom been? Haven't seen her in weeks

JANELLE: Lucky 4 U. I saw her yesterday. You guys are on opposite schedules—count your blessings...she seems to be worse lately

I put my phone down, and cross off number two on the list. Now it's time to shut my mind down and go to sleep. I take out my gun and place it under my pillow. As I'm dozing, I think I can still smell Vincent on me. I put my arm up to my nose and inhale as deeply as possible, but the scent disappeared. My body is under so much stress that within mere moments, I'm completely asleep.

Somewhere in the recesses of my sleeping mind, I hear the front door open and shut. My bedroom light flicks on and Janelle jumps into my bed. "Eve! Wake up!" Her hands are on me and she shakes me awake.

I sit up in a shock and my heart skips a beat. When I see it's Janelle, I blink a few times, my eyes adjusting to the light.

"You don't know—I have to tell you—holy shit! Eve!"

"What? What happened?" My voice is raspy and sounds strangled. Janelle's eyes are wide and she's...smiling? I rub my eyes.

"You don't understand, Eve! It was epic!"

"Huh? What the hell is going on?" I look at the time and see that it's two am.

"I was in the Meatpacking district tonight. There were fights on, but it was a really small thing. Not like the gigantic crowd I took you to." I shrug my shoulders and rub my eyes again, still trying to get my body to understand that it's awake now.

"All of a sudden, the announcer tells us that the Bull is fighting. He wasn't on the roster."

When I hear his name, my heart stutters in my chest.

"He got in the center of the circle, looking angry as hell. And PS, angry Bull is like the hottest man on the planet! It should be illegal to look that good." She fans her face and I resist the urge to roll my eyes. "But forget that." She waves her hand around as if to push the thought away. She still doesn't know that Vincent is the Bull. And that Vincent is…Vincent. But now isn't the time to mention it. I need to hear the entire story.

"Okay—so…?" I'm waiting for her to continue.

"So, he gets into the ring. Angry. Somehow, Carlos, YOUR Carlos, gets thrown inside." My eyes feel like they're bugging out of my skull.

She pushes her hair back with her hands. "So, Carlos gets pushed into the ring, looking around like a deer in motherfucking headlights!"

"Oh. My. God." My stomach turns and I feel like I may throw up.

Janelle's smile is practically splitting her face apart. She gets back out of bed, jumping up and down like she just won the lotto. "The Bull tears off his shirt in the middle of the circle, Eve! Not normal-like, but like a man enraged! The entire place was going berserk!"

Janelle paces the room, her excitement so huge that sitting isn't possible. "Carlos's fear disappears, and he looks like he's going to tear the Bull's head off! Clearly, there is some shit between them…"

"Wait. C-Carlos?" I can barely say his name.

"Yes, Eve. Are you lis-ten-ing? Carlos! Sergeant of Arms for the Snakes. The same fucker who tried to rape you, Eve. The same Carlos! Are you awake?

I swallow hard, my voice sounding panicked. "And?"

"And the Bull went apeshit. I've never seen him fight like this. Normally he does what he has to do and has some fun. He always wins, obviously, but gives everyone a little show first. This time? It was total annihilation. At first, everyone was yelling, excited even. After three minutes, it was silence. It looked like he broke every bone in Carlos's body!"

"Wait. What? My voice is monotone; my mind in so much shock it can barely process what she's telling me.

"YES! No one was stopping him! The announcer stood there in silence, letting the Bull do whatever the hell he wanted. At one point, Carlos was a heap of blood on the floor. His nose was totally shattered. I saw his arms were both bent in a crazy direction. The Bull literally, like, publically humiliated him and broke that motherfucker, limb by mother-fucking limb!"

Laughter starts to bubble up inside my chest. I'm in a state of complete shock and apparently, this is my body's reaction. Janelle joins me, and somehow, we're laughing our asses off! Tears are pouring down her face from glee.

"Carlos had to be carried out by two bouncers and probably dropped off at the hospital! It was the scariest thing I had ever seen. In. My. Life. He may be dead! And when the Bull was finished? Oh. My. God, Eve! When the Bull was finished, he spit on Carlos's body, picked up his shirt, and walked out of the circle like it was just another goddamn day!"

"But, what…" I'm shaking my head, still in disbelief.

"You obviously have a guardian angel, Eve. I mean, he's gone! Carlos is done! God, I can't wait to tell everyone!" She kisses me on the forehead and skips into the bathroom, leaving me alone in our bedroom.

I shut my eyes, not sure how to deal with this new development when my throat starts to burn. I let the tears flow. I'm free.

CHAPTER 16

I've gone back and forth a million times in my head over it, but I think that it's probably best this way. If he wanted to reach out to me, he would have. He has my number.

On a daily basis, my mind goes through something like this:

"He killed, or almost killed, someone in my honor. What am I supposed to do, call him and thank him?"

"Holy shit—Vincent is a killer! I can't be friends with a killer!"

"I'm being crazy. Vincent is amazing. Vincent is perfect for me."

"No—a man like Vincent isn't perfect for me. He's dangerous, and I have plans for myself. Big plans, including college and grad school and a big job!"

"But if not for Vincent, I might have been killed by now. Or raped. Or who knows. The man saved my life. And more than anything...I miss him."

"I've never had anyone in my life understand me bone-deep like that. I know I'm young, but something tells me that he is IT. He is the one. I'm trying to ignore the nagging feeling that Vincent is love, but it won't stop knocking on my heart."

I drop my head in my hands, sick of my thoughts. I need to focus right now on finishing off my year well and praying on getting into college. My phone chimes, shaking me out of my obsessing. I check the text and see it's Ms. Levine asking me to call her. When I get her on the phone, she tells me to come over—she has good news for me!

Right before I can head out, my mom struts into the apartment, teetering and swaying on high heels.

"Well, if it isn't my second daughter," she slurs. Her makeup is smeared and the blond highlights in her hair have grown out, leaving a limp brown line at her roots. For a woman who is obsessed with appearances, I'm shocked she looks so unkempt. She steps closer to me, her voice lowering as if she wants to tell me a secret. "I haven't seen you in quite some time, huh? You're not avoiding me, right?"

"No. I guess our schedules have just been—"

"Don't talk back to me!" She screams. I instantly drop my head, knowing that when she's at this point in her mental state, nothing but silence will do.

Her breaths shortens, and she starts huffing. "One of the girls at the club told me that she heard from Angelo that you applied to college!" She starts to laugh as if it's a big joke. "I told her that there is no goddamned way you did. You wouldn't go against my wishes, would you, Eve?" She steps closer to me as I move backward to avoid her. "My own daughter. My own flesh and blood wouldn't do that to me, right? Not when you know that we need you to work full time. Not when you know that we need the money!" Her voice is shrill and I can feel my heart pick up its pace. "…Not when you know that you should have dropped out of school years ago!" she says with a scream.

Before I think about what I should say, the words come tumbling out of my mouth. "Mom, you're wrong. It's only a few more years of time. And imagine the job I could get! So much more money!"

"WHAT?" Her shriek can probably be heard around the entire floor. "I'll kill you! I brought you into the world and I have every right to take you out of it! I owe people money and I need you to bring some in for me!"

I blink hard, understanding finally dawning on me. At the end of the day, my mom is a selfish and jealous woman who has absolutely zero care about me; all she knows is what she wants. After everything that's happened in my eighteen years of life, I simply can't let her hold me down anymore. I just can't keep hoping that one day she'll change. It's enough already! Somehow, the truth after all these years becomes obvious. If I want to move on out of the Blue Houses, I've got to move on from her. I need to stop hoping and wishing that she'll eventually become a real mother to me and just focus on my own path. She's not on my side and she never will be.

She raises her hand to hit me and I duck, running out the apartment door. She turns around, yelling, "EVE! YOU GET FUCKING BACK HERE!" Her voice is a high-pitched screech. Instead of stopping, I open up the stairwell and go flying down the steps.

Before I get to the first floor, I see George in a corner with his usual bottle of whiskey. "Hey, Eve. In a rush?" I stop myself, breathing heavy, but manage to put my hand in my purse to pull out a dollar bill.

"I hear you're going to college," he says as he takes the dollar, the unmistakable shine of pride in his eyes.

"Yeah, I hope so. I'm waiting to hear back." I shrug, still catching my breath and looking up the steps, trying to hear if my mother is following me down.

"Don't give up, okay? Irina... don't listen to her. You're going to go places. I know it. Knew it since you were a little kid." I nod my head, surprised by his comment.

179

His voice is scratchy. "Hurry. If she comes down here, I'll tell her I didn't see you," he says with a wink.

I can't help the smile that forms on my face. "Thanks, George. I'll see you soon, okay?" I leave the Blue Houses and jog to the subway.

I jump on the train uptown, heart thudding. Twenty minutes later, I get into Ms. Levine's building and race to the elevators, ignoring the door attendant calling out to me. When I get to her floor, I rush to her door and knock hard. She opens up and engulfs me in her arms.

"Columbia accepted you! You're in!" We both jump together, embracing. I do a happy dance, my arms up in the air.

"Come in!" She pushes some forms toward me as I step into her foyer. "Full scholarship! Grants to cover living expenses and books! Get these signed by your mom..." She hands me pages of documents and winks, walking to the bathroom. I take my shoes off, leaving them by the door. Sitting at her dining table, I pull a pen out of my bag and quickly sign where necessary, forging my mom's signature without blinking an eye. At this point, nothing would stop me from accepting admission.

A few minutes later, she walks back into the room. "You wouldn't believe this, Ms. Levine, but while you were in the bathroom, my mom came over. Signed all these documents. Then ran out!"

She shakes her head and chuckles at me, but takes the forms nonetheless.

A sense of relief comes over me as I realize I'm finally taking my life into my own hands. Before I can enjoy the feeling, a deep sense of anxiety settles into my chest. The truth is, I'm worried. What if I don't fit in? What if I get there and can't handle the workload? I peer at my loose, holey jeans and large shirt from Goodwill. I'm obviously going to have to put a mask on in order to blend into this school. Or maybe, I'll have to take off my mask?

I've been covering up for so long, I'm not even really sure who the "real me" is anymore.

"Ms. Levine, I want you to know how thankful I am for everything you've done for me." I tuck my feet under my butt, and she seems to immediately sense my discomfort.

"Of course! But what's wrong?" She squints, tilting her head to the side and sitting beside me.

I lick my lips, clasping my hands together. I know I should confide in her. She is, after all, the only person I know who has ever even been to college. "What if I don't belong there?" I ask. She gives me a half smile as if she was waiting for me to bring this up. "I know that I live in the city with all different kinds of people. But these kids have never been inside a classroom that makes them nervous for their lives. I know that most of them will come from the best prep schools. They can barely fathom the concept of their lives being up for grabs."

"Yes," she says, clicking her tongue. "They are quite different from what you're used to. But you have this opportunity, and I want you to take advantage of it. I don't want you to shrink back. When you're there, shed the fear and insecurity, and put on confidence. As I always say, turn the fear you harbor into resilience and make it all count. You deserve this opportunity, Eve. More than anyone else, you deserve this."

Self-doubt continues to plague me, despite her confidence in me.

She grabs my hand, forcing me to face her. "You'll have to stop wearing hats and your hood over your head. You can start to wear clothes that are more fitting for a girl. You're stunning, Eve. And it's not easy for you to hide. Think of it this way. When you get to Columbia, you don't have to try to hide yourself. You can be the gorgeous and intelligent girl you actually are! I want you to finally be free. Sure, some of those kids will be assholes. But that's part of life, right?"

I think about Vincent for a moment and his upper-crust life. Tears threaten, but I hold them back and focus on what's in front of me. Columbia. Maybe one day, after I graduate, I'll be able to, with confidence, look a man like Vincent in the eye and feel deserving of his time.

I still haven't told Janelle anything about Vincent. Maybe I should tell Ms. Levine. Not everything, but just some parts. I feel lost after what happened with him, and I'm still unsure why things turned out the way they did.

"Actually, there's something I wanted to talk to you about. There's kind of been a guy. But he's sort of ghosted out on me. And I'm not really sure what to do about it..."

"Okay," she says anxiously. "Go on."

I give her the general details of what happened, nothing sexual or detailed about Carlos, either, and ask her what she thinks.

She stares at me apprehensively. "Something sounds a little fishy about this whole thing, Eve. You've looked him up, right?"

I click my tongue for a second. "Uh, no, I haven't." I turn my head to the side, attempting to avoid her intelligent gaze.

"Eve," she snaps. "You gotta get on a computer and check him out. Is he on Facebook? How can you just go off with him? You met him at some underground fight, got into his car, let him take you out to eat, and you don't even know his last name?" Her voice is skeptical as if she can't believe my naiveté.

I swallow. "Yeah, okay, I'll look him up." The moment the words leave my mouth, I realize that I don't want to know more about him. I'm afraid to uncover something that I won't like. I just want to stay in this little bubble I've created for myself. There's definitely something different about Vincent. But then again, I'm used to seeing aggressive men. Plus, he's obviously rich.

That's all it is, right? Okay sure, so he almost killed someone on my behalf. But he's a fighter. He did it to help me. He isn't connected to anyone or anything. Well, at least I think he isn't. His family is in business.

She takes my hands in hers. "You must be careful, Eve. Don't bury your head in the sand. I'm glad he's been decent to you so far, but even the fact that he just comes and goes of his own accord—randomly working out near your pawnshop—nothing is near that pawnshop! Drives this fancy car? Something smells wrong here. He's got *gang* written all over him." Her voice is apprehensive.

I take my hands out from hers feeling agitated by her questions. "There's no way he's gang affiliated. He's too rich and powerful for that."

"Eve, we both know that not all gangs are roaming the streets. Maybe he's a dealer?" I think for a moment, but Vincent is too sophisticated for that.

"Well, I know him now. Maybe not his blood type or his last name, but I've spent a lot of time with him and he's been nothing but respectful. He isn't like the other gang guys I know. Or even dealers." I shake my head vehemently. "Not at all."

I imagine the gangbangers I know from the Snakes and the Cartel. At heart, those guys are chaos. Disorganized. Street smart. Book stupid. Vincent is nothing like them. Nothing at all.

When Ms. Levine sees my mind operating, she lets out a breath and gets up, pulling out an old laptop of hers. "Eve, promise me that you'll go home and look him up. I want you to keep this computer for school anyway, okay? Now that you have this, you don't have any excuse not to know."

I hug her tight. "Thank you for everything."

"You make me so proud, Eve. Truly. Now, get your stuff together! Summer classes start in June, right after graduation!"

After lots of hugs, I get on the subway and head downtown. Walking through my front door, I go straight into my bathroom and look in the mirror. Pushing thoughts of Vincent out of my head for the millionth time, I tell myself that my life is about to change for the better. I can't wipe the smile off my face when I realize I'm starting Columbia. Ahhh!

I turn my head for a moment, staring at the computer Ms. Levine gave me. I decide that I don't want to look him up. I'm not ready to learn anything more than I already know. And really, who knows if I'll ever even see him again. He hasn't reached out to me, and I'm too chicken to text him again. So, it doesn't matter who he is or isn't, right?

I swallow back my sadness, realizing I'm hung up on a guy who hasn't been in touch with me for weeks. A guy whose last name I don't even know. A guy who is technically a killer. I hope he doesn't go to jail for this. Oh my God. How could I not even have considered the legal implications of what Vincent did? If it gets back to the cops that he killed Carlos, he could go to jail. Or even worse, maybe the Snakes are going to try to retaliate against him! I blink hard a few times and try to breathe. Should I warn him? I told him all about Carlos and the Snakes and he didn't seem surprised at all. He's also not stupid. He must have considered the ramifications of what he did, right?

Luckily, Janelle comes home and my mind is instantly occupied with good thoughts. We celebrate my admission by ordering Domino's thin-crust pizza and cheesy bread and dancing to Drake.

Eventually, she lowers the music and we drop onto the couch. I turn to her. "What the hell are we going to tell Mom about school?"

"Ugh, who cares?" Janelle says nonchalantly, throwing her bare feet up onto the coffee table with a smile on her face. "She's hardly home, anyway. We'll tell her you've got a new boyfriend and you're staying with him. Since you've got grants and scholarships covering everything, there shouldn't be a money trail." Janelle does an evil-sounding laugh and I join in, as if we're conspiring to take over the world. And maybe in some ways, we are. Moments later, we erupt into genuine laughter, feeling high over the fact that college is now no longer a pipe dream, but an actuality.

CHAPTER 17

The school year goes on uneventfully, finally ending in a blur of standardized testing and Advanced Placement exams. I am the valedictorian, and I make a simple speech at the graduation ceremony about perseverance and never giving up in life, no matter the odds. While I'm embarrassed to speak in public, I'm surprised the amount of pride I feel standing up there. It may only be the old gymnasium in my high school, but getting to this point means something to me. When I'm finished, the audience and other students clap politely while Janelle screams like crazy. With a red face, I walk away from the podium and take my seat. It's hot as hell in here; the air conditioning must be broken. I press the long blue gown to my chest, trying to soak up the sweat.

I turn to the students next to me when it finally dawns on me that hardly anyone I started with during my freshman year is sitting with me now. Out of two hundred and fifty students from my freshman class, it looks like only about one hundred kids are graduating. I guess the rest all dropped out or got their GED certificates. I know that technically, I saw it all unfold. I mean, I lived it. I watched as boys who were my friends as children grew up and joined gangs. I don't believe they were looking for bloodshed, at least, not at first. They just wanted to belong. Understandably, they looked for protection on the street and some respect from their peers. Isn't that all it is? Can I fault them for that?

I look out into the audience, seeing some Blue House families gathered together with pride. Janelle's face stands out among them all; she's staring at me, glowing with joy. It hurts me that she never got to graduate, but at the same time, I know I'm doing this for both of us. The reality is—without her support, I never could have made it to this point. I drop my head for a moment and say a little prayer to God, thanking Him for giving me my sister. As usual, Vincent's face comes into my head. I drop a line of thanks for him too. Because without him, I'd probably be dead by now. He may have only popped into my life for a short period of time, but damn did he manage to come at just the time I needed him most.

When the graduation is over, Ms. Levine takes Janelle and me out for a surprise celebration lunch. We drive down into the Flatiron district and I see the restaurant. My throat tightens. We're at Eataly, where Vincent picked up sandwiches for us all those months ago while we skated in Central Park. I walk inside, trying to keep cool as fancy-looking people walk with baskets full of fresh fettuccini and gelato. I see a line of people waiting for fresh cannoli. The entire place is like a vibrant marketplace straight out of my dreams.

I thought I was doing okay without hearing from him, that I could just take his help with Carlos and all the emotions he brought out of me and box them up in a quiet part of my brain. But the moment I see those special sandwiches on display, I have to swallow back my tears.

Ms. Levine seems to notice my distress. "Don't you like it here? The restaurant is just around the corner over there." She points to a perfect spot that is roped off: Riso e Risoto. "I thought you would..." Her voice trails off as her face scrunches up as if I've upset her.

Janelle looks at me, confused. This is one of the coolest restaurants right now, and I know that I'm so lucky to be here. They're probably sensing my unease and imagine me to be ungrateful. Meanwhile, nothing could be further from the truth.

I shake my head, needing to say something to let them know how thankful I am. "No. I absolutely love it. I-I can't thank you enough for bringing me here. I guess I'm just nervous for college to begin." I shrug.

She clicks her tongue, draping an arm around me in a motherly gesture. We walk into the restaurant where a beautiful and young hostess immediately seats us.

"Don't worry, Eve." We take our seats. "You should be excited! Everyone is nervous at first, but just wait until it all begins!"

While we all scan our menus, the waiter takes our drink orders. We chat about move-in dates and signing up for classes. I already got my room assignment, and apparently, I'm living with a girl from Texas.

Janelle looks at me, a huge smile on her face. "Eve, there's something I wanna tell you."

"What's up?" I take a sip of my soda, my mouth around the straw while I look up at her.

"Well, you know I only stayed at the Blue Houses because you were still there. Now that you're moving out, I decided I'm going to rent a place with some girls from the salon. It's a small place in midtown, but—"

"Janelle!" I jump out of my chair and run to hers. She stands up and we embrace. Our lives are really changing. We're truly moving on! Ms. Levine turns to us both, grinning.

The waiter comes back and I order a risotto with honeynut squash, sage, and black truffle butter. Janelle and Ms. Levine agree that it sounds great, and decide to order the same.

Ms. Levine turns to me. "Don't forget, Eve. With your full scholarship and grant money, your only job is to maintain a 3.2 GPA and to enjoy life for a change. If you want extra cash, there are work-study programs like the library help desk."

I smile broadly in excitement.

We finish our delicious food—and holy shit is it amazing—and then hug and kiss Ms. Levine goodbye. Janelle and I take the bus together back to the Blue Houses. Now that Carlos is dead, the Cartel seems to have risen in power and the fighting seems to be slowing down.

We walk into our quiet apartment that we'll both be moving out of soon enough. Janelle pulls out a bottle of vodka from the freezer and some seltzer water from the fridge. After cutting up a few lemons, she makes us drinks. Handing me a glass, I take it happily. We're alone at home, and I have nothing to worry about with Janelle by my side.

She raises her cup in a toast. "You're gonna go to college. There are gonna be frat parties and stuff. You've got to know what it's like to be wasted in a comfortable environment."

I laugh at her comment. "And anyway," she continues, "I want to say that I'm proud of you. I'm so happy right now. To our futures!"

"To getting out of this hell hole!" I add.

"To moving on and up!"

We clink our glasses together and moments later, ask for another. By our third, I'm swaying as I walk to the bathroom.

After I'm done peeing, I realize that I miss Vincent so much my chest aches. In fact, it hurts even more now than ever. I thought drinking was supposed to make me forget?

I'm washing my hands and staring at myself in the mirror, becoming angry. Why am I being such a baby about him? Why can't I go ahead and text him? I mean, I'm all about women's lib! He doesn't have to reach out first. I take out my phone and find his name in my contacts. *There he is!*

ME: Hey Vincent. Hi!!! Where are you???

I blink a few times when I see the dots show up, letting me know he's about to reply. "Oh my God, he's going to reply!" I jump up and down, squealing.

VINCENT: Are you okay? Do you need me?

ME: Yupppp all's well. Just home with my sister….

VINCENT: Ah, that's good. What are you girls up to?

ME: Just drinkin' too much :-)

VINCENT: I see. So, this is a drunken text, huh?

ME: Yupppp. Why haven't you called me?

VINCENT: Been busy.

ME: Of course MR. FANCIEST PANTS ON EARTH

I laugh out loud to myself, thinking I'm the funniest person ever. Why did I never realize before how funny I am?

VINCENT: Hah. Not that fancy…

I roll my eyes.

ME: Not fancy my ass!!!

VINCENT: =-)

I huff. What is that supposed to mean? Stupid emoji. Behind my eyes, all I can see is his stupidly perfect smile, and I suddenly feel the urge to wipe it off his face! I've been waiting for him. Pining, for fuck's sake! And he's what, smiling with an emoji! The NERVE!

ME: You're an asshole!!!

"There!" I huff out loud.

VINCENT: ???

ME: You heard me. You think you can just waltz into my life and then waltz out? Who the hell do you think you are?

My heart pounds. I can't even believe him right now. And he isn't even replying! I deserve a reply. I'm a human being, too!

ME: Ah, now you don't reply? I'm not good enough for your perfect world? Well guess what! I'm going to college! Starting summerrrrr! And I'm gonna be someone! And one day you'll see me and I'll be like, I'm busy motha-fucka!!!!

I slide down on the floor of the bathroom. Minutes pass, and he still hasn't replied. Why won't he respond? I feel nauseous.

ME: I hate you!

I turn my phone off and the tears start to fall. I'm crying. Did I do something wrong? Is the room spinning?

"Yo, Eve." Janelle walks into the bathroom. "What's wrong?" I screw my eyes closed but can hear the concern in her voice.

"Nothing. Juuuust …" I try to speak, but nothing is coming out right.

"All right, you little drunkard. I think you've had enough. She opens the bathroom cabinet, pulling out a bottle of Advil and filling a cup with water from the sink. She hands the pills to me with the water and somehow, I swallow it down.

Lifting me off the ground, she practically drags me to my bed. "Now go pass out and I'll see you in the morning. Leo is calling, I'm gonna go spend the night." She tucks me under my covers.

All I can think about is Vincent. And how much I hate his face. I hate his brain. I hate his huge gorgeous warm body that makes me feel insane things. I hate how he always carries me around and it feels like home. His intelligence. I hate how he looks at me like I matter. Like, I mean something to him. I love him. I love him so much.

I cry harder into my pillow until I finally pass out.

I wake up the next morning with a pounding head. It feels like someone is hammering into my skull. I turn around and see Janelle's bed is still empty. The clock says it's six in the morning. What the hell? Why am I up so damn early? I slowly stand, my hand pressing against the wall for balance as I go to use the bathroom. I drop my head in my hands while sitting on the toilet seat, trying to soothe the ache when I spot my cell phone on the floor. I pick it up and turn it back on.

Oh shit. Oh shit, shit, motherfucking shit! What did I do? I read my texts to Vincent and I want to die of shame. I have to fix this!

ME: Hey. Sorry about the texts... was drunk, not sure what came over me.

I close the phone, realizing that there is no way in hell he's gonna reply at this hour. But when my phone buzzes, I turn around and grab it.

VINCENT: It's ok. We're cool, Eve. And congrats on school. You deserve it.

I want to reply. Hell, I want to talk to him. I want to see him. I turn on the shower and get under the spray. First, shower. Second, coffee. Then I'll figure out how to reply.

But after I'm done with all that, I stare at my phone and feel the nerves fluttering in my stomach. His last comment wasn't exactly asking for a reply, right? Maybe he doesn't want to hear from me. I mean, if I were him, I wouldn't want to hear from me after last night. I re-read my texts to him, feeling more embarrassed each time.

I remember the new book I took out of the library is in my backpack. If I read it, maybe it'll relax me. Then, I can decide what to do.

I'm shaken out of my book-induced trance when Janelle walks in with a huge box in her arms. "Hey girl, this came for you." She has her phone on her ear as she drops the box on my bed before walking out of the room.

I glance at the clock and see that it's already three o'clock in the afternoon! Going into the kitchen, I take a knife from a drawer and bring it back into my bedroom. I jump onto my bed and lean over the box in excitement, slicing the taped seam with relish.

I open it quickly as if it were Christmas. A beautiful travel coffee mug in pink, a cozy sweatshirt that says: COLLEGE, a pair of warm Ugg slippers with fur inside that I guess I can wear around the dorms! I slide them on and they fit perfectly. There are six packages of beautiful fountain pens, and four spiral notebooks, with dividers. Sticky pads! Whoever did this, obviously went to town at Staples and holy shit, I'm not complaining! I pull out a scientific calculator. Wow! I open up an envelope and see a gift card to Barnes and Noble for $500.00. What! I guess I can use this when I need to buy books! I keep rummaging through, and see a box of Kind bars! I guess they will be useful when I'm running between classes. My heart is pounding with excitement. College is coming! I need to call Ms. Levine. She's the best!

When I finally empty the box, I grab my phone and with shaking fingers, dial her number.

"Hey Eve!" Her voice is happiness.

"Oh my God! I can't believe what you sent me. SO amazing, I'm freaking out!" My words come out in a rush.

"Uh, Eve. I'm sorry, but I didn't send you anything."

"Wait, what?" My heart beats erratically as my eyes zero in on all the goodies on my bed.

"What did you get?" she asks probingly.

I breathe silently over the line. No. It couldn't be. "Oh, um, okay…Ms. Levine. I'll, um, call you back." I hang up the phone quickly and go through the box again.

I put my head in my hands and realize that I can't ignore this. It's too much. Too…thoughtful. Damn him!

ME: Hey

VINCENT: Hey you. I assume you got the package?

ME: How can I thank you? It's too much

VINCENT: No. It's not enough.

ME: It really means more than you know. Truly. I wish I could do something back

VINCENT: When you finish college and get into law school, that'll be my thank you. Don't give up. Focus. And don't party too hard.

ME: Thanks, Daddy… I'll be moving on June 23. Should I write it on one of my new Post-Its and leave it on the kitchen table as a re-minder?

VINCENT: Daddy, huh? :-)

I roll my eyes, but smile so hard my face hurts.

ME: Thanks, friend

VINCENT: My pleasure, baby. Kick ass and good luck.

I lay on my bed with all my stuff around me. Janelle and I are both plan-ning to pack our things together in the next week. She'll help me move, and I'll help her as well. Being so close to home has its perks.

"Vincent," I say loudly. I want him so badly, but I also know that he is staying away from me for a reason. Maybe it's for the best. And I've got an entire life to live, right? I know that until I reach my goals, I'll never feel confident or comfortable around him. I'll always be afraid that he just sees me as some nobody. I need to fix myself before I can be confident enough to be with a man like him. Maybe it's best that he backed off. And like he said, I've got to focus now, anyway. I've got to get my head in the game! It's time to accomplish my goals.

I stand up and decide to start packing my things. One more week! College, here I come.

CHAPTER 18

Two Months Later

I've kept my word. My life is about more than first love...if you could even call it that. I have goals and right now, my education comes first.

Columbia is awesome. It's everything I could have ever hoped for and then some. I did the six-week summer session to get a jump-start on classes. A few girls in my dorm arrived early too, and we've all instantly clicked. a

Ms. Levine and Janelle ended up surprising me with a shopping trip to some decent consignment stores, so I finally dress like an eighteen-year-old woman, not a fourteen-year-old boy hiding in baggy clothes. After enduring almost two decades of hell in the Blue Houses, I finally feel like I could fit in. This is my place; this is where I'm trying to belong.

The summer heat is still stifling, but most of the students are finally on campus. I came with my friends from my dorm; we're walking through the extracurricular activities fair, moving from booth to booth and jotting our names down for random activities. Debate Club. Model Congress. Finally, I found myself at the PanHellenic Counsel table, filled with information about the sororities on campus. The girl sitting down, her name-tag says: CLAIRE, seems pretty cool. Her hair is braided in a 1960s flower-child way, and she's wearing a long and flowy blue dress.

I sign my name down for sorority rush while Claire asks me some questions. We chat for a few minutes about prospective majors, and it turns out we're both pre-law.

"Actually, I'm supposed to meet up at eleven-thirty with some girls from my sorority for lunch. Why don't you join us?" I'm unsure what to make of this. Sororities aren't really my thing. But before I could think too much about it, I blurt out, "Yes, I'd love that actually."

"How about we meet at the Coffee Cup at eleven-fifteen and we'll walk together to the dining hall? By the way, we're in Phi Alpha." She winks like she just let me in on a secret.

"Okay, cool. I'll see you there." I give her a soft smile and say goodbye.

I find the girls to tell them I'm leaving for class. The rest of the morning moves quickly. Tons of work gets assigned, and I'm anxious to get started.

I meet Claire outside of the Coffee Cup as planned. We walk side by side through campus, discussing our schedules for the spring semester. Luckily, she talks a lot. She tells me all about her sorority, and I'm trying to keep up with all the parties and fun they apparently have together.

We walk into the dining hall that has turned into chaos. Over the summer, it was pretty quiet with no one other than jocks and kids taking summer classes. But now, with most of the students back on campus, it's frenzied.

The two of us wait in the lunch line and talk about bands we like. Turns out we have really similar taste in music. Our energy is connecting, and I'm actually feeling really good. Maybe joining a sorority would be a good thing for me.

"Do you play any sports?" She's looking straight ahead, getting annoyed that the line seems to have frozen to a standstill.

"Nah, I'm more of the bookworm type." I may want to hide where I come from, but my lies end there.

She looks me up and down. "Ugh, I hate girls like you who just wake up with a body to kill." She rolls her eyes at me playfully. "I play volleyball. Tryouts are coming up, and I really want to make the varsity team this year."

"With your height, I don't doubt it. You're probably awesome." I didn't realize when she was sitting down, but Claire looks like she's even taller than Janelle.

She points to some sandwiches underneath a little heater-looking thing. "Oh, the chicken sandwiches here are the best!" I watch as she takes one and I go ahead and pick one up as well, grabbing a bottle of water to go with it. The sandwich is warm and I can't wait to dig in. We leave the line after paying and carry our lunch trays to the seating area while she looks around, trying to find her friends.

"There they are!" she exclaims, walking to the left. I follow her and take a seat beside her. All of her friends at the table are smiling and dressed similarly in blue jeans and collared shirts. I'm in Pleasantville!

"Hey guys, this is Eve. I met her during the extracurricular fair!"

They all look me up and down and say polite hellos. Claire goes around the table introducing them to me. A few of them are sophomores like her, and two of them are juniors. I give a small wave to everyone, feeling really nervous by their inquisitive gazes. I sit down and unwrap my chicken sandwich, realizing at that moment how hungry I am.

Ms. Levine made sure the school gave me a food credit. I can eat anything in the dining hall at any time—it's like my personal pantry. Pretty nice of the school to take care of me like this, but Ms. Levine always says that you can't get what you don't ask for. Now here I am, eating like a queen in the best school in the country, all for free. Life is good!

I'm taking a bite out of my food when I feel a presence. I'm obviously not the only one, because the noise level seems to have quieted down and as I look up; I notice that everyone has their heads turned toward the front doors. I follow the collective gaze, wondering what they're looking at.

That's when I see him.

He's just so much taller and bigger than everyone else. He's a man among boys. My jaw actually drops when I take him in. He has a few girls giggling behind him, and guys on either side. What. The. Fuck.

"Wow," Claire says in a breathy voice, momentarily shaking me out of my thoughts.

Allison sees the look of shock on my face and takes it upon herself to fill me in. "Oh, that's Vincent Borignone. He's a god around here. I would say you'll get used to him with time, but no one ever does. He's just that insanely sexy. Brilliant! And he's also one of the most connected people you'll ever meet. Some people say that he's the son of the infamous Antonio Borignone. Like, you know, the crime family. But that's probably just a rumor—"

I lift a hand, stopping her. "Wait, w-what?" The name Vincent Borignone echoes in my ear. Rumor. It's a rumor. I never knew his last name. Suddenly, it all clicks—all the puzzle pieces falling into place. It's him. He never told me his last name because he's a mafia prince! And he goes here. To Columbia. To MY school. Where my future is supposed to be happening. My mind is working on overtime right now. I blink, staring out into space while my heart beats into my throat.

Claire turns to me, shaking me out of my fog. "Well, goddamn! It's only been a few months, but he's even better looking now. The man just gets hotter with age." They all start laughing.

"Eve, are you okay?" Claire asks, putting her hand on my back.

I slowly turn toward her, plastering a fake smile on my face. "Is he in a fraternity?" I squeak, trying to move the conversation forward.

"No way! But he doesn't need to be in one; he just goes where he wants, and I swear, it's like the entire student body rolls out the red carpet for him. He can get into any party at any time."

I bring my bottle of water to my lips when Allison points to his table. "By the way, that's Daniela." My body freezes at the mention of a girl in connection with Vincent; the water I was just swallowing moves down the wrong pipe—I'm choking. Claire taps my back as I cough like crazy. "Oh my God, are you okay?" I clear my throat, trying to regain my composure.

One of Claire's friends, I think her name is Jen, starts talking. "Daniela is such a bitch. She's gorgeous, and no one knows it better than her. Of course, she's in O Chi A…that's the slutty sorority, FYI."

We all turn as a unit to stare at their table when Jen starts up again. "She's always up Vincent's ass. But I'd bet he messes around on her all the time. Last year, Jillian Samson said she gave him a blow job—" She keeps talking, but my mind has gone static.

He has a girlfriend? Holy shit. And she's gorgeous. Actually, I remember her from the fight the first night Vincent and I met. The redhead. She moves from her own seat onto his lap, wrapping a pale, skinny arm around his back with a smile on her face. Her hands move to his hair; he looks relaxed but disinterested. She puts her lips near his ear for a moment and then looks around the room, making sure that we all see she's with him. I want to scream and cry right now. Instead, I take a slow sip of my water, keeping my face as neutral as I can while I continue to watch. No wonder he didn't want more with me. He already has someone, and she looks like she just walked out of *Vogue* magazine.

Vincent Borignone. My life just got a hell of a lot more complicated.

ACKNOWLEDGMENTS

I am indebted to the following people for their help and support:
To Jon, I love you through and through.

To my kids and Lina, for being patient while I write.

To Billi Joy Carson at Editing Addict, you aren't just an editor but also a partner and a friend. Your moral support is simply invaluable. You're also just a brilliant editor, who managed to turn my story into something I never dreamed it could be. Thank you really isn't enough. You're a #goddamngenius for sure !

To Ellie at LoveNBooks, for squeezing me into your hectic schedule and for taking a chance on an unknown author. You took my first manuscript and gave me THE edit that turned my book into something truly viable. I am forever grateful.

To Autumn at Wordsmith Publicity, thank you for helping me get this labor of love off the ground and dealing with my mania.

To Sarah at Okay Creations for the killer cover.

To my Beta readers: Lauren, who read those earliest drafts and believed in me. Candice, who has been on this journey since day one. To Leigh, there's no other way to describe this book except to say that it was a partnership—with you. Andrea at Hot Tree Editing, thank you for your kickass beta read! Jana, Jayme, Ronna, Amee and Roxy, your feedback was essential! Thank you!

Tuxedo Park Library
227 Route 17 Box 776
Tuxedo Park, NY 10987
(845)351-2207
www.tuxedoparklibrary.org

74445551R00115

Made in the USA
Middletown, DE
25 May 2018